The Ob

Ai

D1650712

About the Book

Observers Aircraft is the indispensable guide to the world's latest aeroplanes and helicopters, and most recent versions of established aircraft types. This, the thirty-eighth annual edition, embraces the latest fixed-wing and variable-geometry aeroplanes and rotorcraft of twenty-four countries. Its scope ranges from such airliner newcomers as the McDonnell Douglas MD-11, Ilyushin Il-96 and Il-114, and Embraer-FAMA CBA-123, through general aviation débutantes, such as the BA-14 Starling, the Avtek 400A, the Laser 300 and the Gulfstream SA-30, and the largest and heaviest freight transport in the world, the An-225 Mriya, to such new or newly-revealed military aircraft as the Lockheed F-117A and Northrop B-2, both of which use stealth technology, and the most ambitious Chinese combat aircraft yet, the XAC H-7. The latest available information is provided on the most recently introduced Soviet military aircraft, such as the Tupolev Tu-160 Blackjack-A strategic bomber, as well as the newest variants of established commercial transports, such as the Boeing 737-500. All data has been checked and revised as necessary, and more than half of the three-view silhouettes are new or have been revised.

About the Author

William Green, compiler of *Observers Aircraft* for 38 years, is internationally known for many works of aviation reference. He entered aviation journalism during the early years of World War II, subsequently serving with the RAF and resuming aviation writing more than 40 years ago, in 1947. William Green is currently managing editor of the monthly *AIR International*, one of the largest-circulation European-based aviation journals, and its thrice-annual companion publication, *AIR Enthusiast*.

The *Observer's* series was launched in 1937 with the publication of *The Observer's Book of Birds*. Today, over fifty years later, paperback *Observers* continue to offer practical, useful information on a wide range of subjects, and with every book regularly revised by experts, the facts are right up-to-date. Students, amateur enthusiasts and professional organisations alike will find the latest *Observers* invaluable.

'Thick and glossy, briskly informative' – *The Guardian*

'If you are a serious spotter of any of the things the series deals with, the books must be indispensable' – *The Times Educational Supplement*

◉ O B S E R V E R S

AIRCRAFT

William Green

With silhouettes by Dennis Punnett

1989/90 edition

FREDERICK WARNE

FREDERICK WARNE

Published by the Penguin Group
27 Wrights Lane, London W8 5TZ, England
Viking Penguin Inc., 40 West 23rd Street, New York, New York 10010, USA
Penguin Books Australia Ltd, Ringwood, Victoria, Australia
Penguin Books Canada Ltd, 2801 John Street, Markham, Ontario, Canada L3R 1B4
Penguin Books (NZ) Ltd, 182–190 Wairau Road, Auckland 10, New Zealand

Penguin Books Ltd, Registered Offices: Harmondsworth, Middlesex, England

Thirty-eighth edition 1989

ISBN 0 7232 3636 4

Typeset, printed and bound in Great Britain by William Clowes Limited, Beccles and
London

INTRODUCTION TO THE 1989 EDITION

THE CLOSING MONTHS of 1988 witnessed the début of two remarkable aircraft: the Soviet An-225 Mriya, by far the largest and heaviest aircraft ever to have flown, and the American B-2, assuredly the most expensive military aircraft ever built. The An-225 special-purpose heavy-lift transport entered flight test mid December and the B-2 strategic bomber employing stealth technology is likely to have flown by the time these words are read. The mid November public roll-out of the latter almost coincided with the first official *admission* of the existence of another aircraft utilising stealth characteristics, the F-117A interdictor, which had, in fact, been flying for more than seven years. The An-225, together with the radical American duo, accordingly can be found in this, the thirty-eighth annual edition of *Observers Aircraft*.

These are by no means the only unconventional shapes that make their first appearance in these pages, however. Others include the X-31A enhanced fighter manoeuvrability demonstrator and a variety of civil débutantes, ranging from the diminutive BA-14 Starling of all-composite construction, via the canarded Avtek 400A and Laser 300 light business aircraft in their definitive forms, to the CBA-123 regional airliner with aft-mounted pusher turboprops. Newcomers of more conventional configuration, include the diminutive SA-30 low-cost business executive transport, the SA-32T trainer, the Il-114 short-haul regional airliner and the 300/400-passenger MD-11, all of which are expected to appear during the year of currency of this volume. Also noteworthy is the growing number of entries relating to Chinese-manufactured aircraft of which the XAC H-7, China's most ambitious indigenous combat aircraft yet, is but the latest.

The year past saw an unprecedented boom in orders for commercial transports, as a comparison of sales figures presented in the following pages with those offered in the last edition of *Observers Aircraft* will clearly reveal. These figures have been updated to the beginning of 1989, as have all data related to aircraft reappearing from previous editions. The accompanying general arrangement silhouette drawings have been meticulously checked for any changes or modifications that may have been applied to the aircraft concerned, and, in this edition, more than half of the drawings are either new or have been revised since they last appeared.   WILLIAM GREEN

AÉROSPATIALE EPSILON

Country of Origin: France.
Type: Tandem two-seat primary/basic trainer.
Power Plant: One 300 hp Textron Lycoming AEIO-540-L1B5D six-cylinder horizontally-opposed engine.
Performance: Max speed, 236 mph (378 km/h) at sea level; max cruise (75% power), 222 mph (358 km/h) at 6,000 ft (1 830 m); max initial climb, 1,850 ft/min (9,4 m/sec); service ceiling, 23,000 ft (7 010 m); endurance (65% power), 3·75 hrs.
Weights: Empty equipped, 2,055 lb (932 kg); max take-off, 2,755 lb (1 250 kg).
Armament: (Export version) Four underwing hardpoints (352-lb/160-kg capacity inboard and 176-lb/80-kg capacity outboard) for practice ordnance. Alternative loads include two twin 7,62-mm gun pods or four six-round 68-mm rocket pods.
Status: Prototypes flown on 22 December 1979 and 12 July 1980. First production Epsilon (against French Air Force requirement for 150) flown 29 June 1983. Four armed Epsilons delivered to Togolese Air Force, and 18 ordered by Portuguese Air Force, of which 17 being assembled by OGMA in Portugal with deliveries commencing 1989.
Notes: Comparable with the ENAER Pillán (see pages 102-3) the Epsilon is used by the French Air Force for the initial phases of the flying syllabus, currently being followed by the CM 170 Magister which is scheduled to be succeeded by the Embraer Tucano from the early 'nineties. The first prototype Epsilon has been re-engined with a 360 shp Turboméca TP 319 turboprop as the Omega (see 1988 edition), this being fundamentally similar to the standard Epsilon aft of the firewall. The Omega flew for the first time on 9 November 1985, and this programme is continuing at the time of closing for press. Manufacture of the Epsilon is sub-contracted to Socata, Aérospatiale's light aircraft subsidiary at Tarbes, which was also responsible for the initial design.

AÉROSPATIALE EPSILON

Dimensions: Span, 25 ft 11¾ in (7,92 m); length, 24 ft 10¾ in (7,59 m); height, 8 ft 8¾ in (2,66 m); wing area, 96·9 sq ft (9,00 m²).

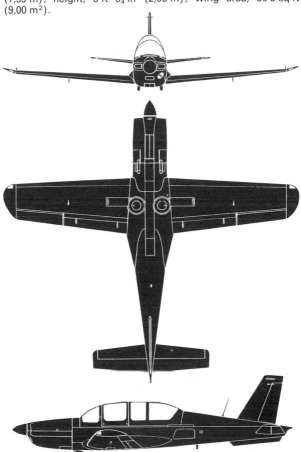

AIRBUS A300-600

Country of Origin: International consortium.
Type: Medium-haul commercial airliner.
Power Plant: Two 56,000 lb st (25 400 kgp) Pratt & Whitney JT9D-7R4H1 or General Electric CF6-80C2 turbofans.
Performance: Max cruise speed, 553 mph (890 km/h) at 25,000 ft (7 620 m); typical long-range cruise, 543 mph (875 km/h) at 31,000 ft (9 450 m); max operating altitude, 40,000 ft (12 200 m); range (with 267 passengers and reserves), 4,272 mls (6 875 km).
Weights: Empty, 172,533 lb (78 260 kg); operational, 191,057 lb (86 662 kg); max take-off, 363,765 lb (165 000 kg).
Accommodation: Flight crew of two, with main cabin seating in six-, seven-, eight- or nine-abreast arrangements, with max capacity for 375 passengers. Typical mixed-class layout offers 28 first class and 239 economy class seats.
Status: First JT9D-powered A300-600 flown on 8 July 1983, and first CF6-powered -600 flying on 20 March 1985. Total of 88 -600s (of 336 A300s of all types) ordered by beginning of 1989, with some 48 delivered and production rate (including A310) running at four monthly.
Notes: The A300, like all members of the Airbus family, is manufactured by a consortium of Aérospatiale (37·9%) of France, Deutsche Airbus (37·9%) of Federal Germany, BAe (20%) of the UK and CASA (4·2%) of Spain. Current production consists of the A300-600 and -600R, the latter being an extended-range version first flown on 9 December 1987. These, with wing improvements, drag-reducing wingtip fences, carbon brakes, upgraded cockpit and latest-technology engines, represent a major advance over the earlier A300B2s and B4s. The -600 is currently available with the 56,000 lb st (25 400 kgp) PW4156 or 59,000 lb st (26 760 kgp) CF6-80C2A1 engines.

AIRBUS A300-600

Dimensions: Span, 147 ft 1¼ in (44,84 m); length, 177 ft 5 in (54,08 m); height, 54 ft 6½ in (16,62 m); wing area, 2,798·7 sq ft (260,00 m²).

AIRBUS A310-300

Country of Origin: International consortium.

Type: Medium-range commercial transport.

Power Plant: Two 52,000 lb st (23 587 kgp) Pratt & Whitney PW4152 or 50,000 lb st (22 680 kgp) General Electric CF6-80C2A2 turbofans.

Performance: Max cruise speed, 557 mph (897 km/h) at 35,000 ft (10 670 m); long-range cruise, 528 mph (850 km/h) at 37,000 ft (11 280 m); range (with 218 passengers and reserves) 5,113 mls (8 228 km) with PW4152 engines, 5,160 mls (8 300 km) with CF6-80C2A2 engines.

Weights: Empty (PW4152) 154,230 lb (69,957 kg), (CF6) 154,360 lb (70 016 kg); max take-off, 330,695 lb (150 000 kg), (optional), 337,305 lb (153 000 kg).

Accommodation: Flight crew of two and max capacity for 280 passengers nine abreast. Typical two-class layout for 20 first class and 198 economy class passengers.

Status: An extended-range version of the basic A310, the A310-300 was first flown on 8 July 1985, with first delivery to launch customer (Swissair) following 17 December 1985. First A310 flown on 3 April 1982, with 176 ordered by beginning of 1989 (of which 90 -300 model) and 140 delivered.

Notes: Second member of the Airbus family to introduce the drag-reducing delta-shaped wingtip fences, the A310-300 differs essentially from earlier versions of the A310 in having an additional fuel tank in the tailplane, being the first production airliner with such. It is also the first production airliner to employ carbonfibre-reinforced plastic for a major structural element (the fin). By comparison with the A300, the A310 has a new wing of reduced size and a shorter fuselage, but retains the basic eight-abreast, twin-aisle fuselage cross section of the earlier aircraft. An additional fuel tank can be installed in part of the cargo hold for increased range.

Dimensions: Span, 144 ft 0 in (43,90 m); length, 153 ft 1 in (46,66 m); height, 51 ft 10 in (15,81 m); wing area, 2,357·3 sq ft (219,00 m²).

AIRBUS A320-200

Country of Origin: International consortium.

Type: Short- to medium-haul commercial transport.

Power Plant: Two 25,000 lb st (11 340 kgp) CFM International CFM56-5-A1 or IAE V2500-A1 turbofans.

Performance: Max cruise speed, 560 mph (903 km/h) at 28,000 ft (8 535 m); range cruise, 520 mph (840 km/h) at 37,000 ft (11 280 m); range (with 150-seat two-class layout and normal reserves, 3,305 mls (5 318 km) with CFM56 engines, 3,270 mls (5 263 km) with V2500 engines.

Weights: Operational empty (CFM56), 87 693 lb (39 777 kg), (V2500) 88,515 lb (40 150 kg); max take-off, 162,040 lb (73 500 kg).

Accommodation: Flight crew of two and seating for up to 179 passengers depending upon layout. A typical two-class layout has 12 first-class seats four abreast and 138 economy-class seats six abreast.

Status: First of four aircraft for flight test programme flown on 22 February 1987. First deliveries (to Air France and British Airways) on 28 and 31 March 1988. First aircraft with IAE V2500 engines flown on 28 July 1988. Production standardised on A320-200 after completion of 21 -100s, and orders totalled 410 aircraft by beginning of 1989, with some 15 delivered. Production rising to 6·5 monthly by end of 1989 and 8·0 monthly by second quarter of 1990.

Notes: The A320-200 differs from the -100 in having additional wing centre section fuel and wingtip fences. A stretched version, the A320-300, is expected to be launched early in 1989, this being some 22·6 ft (6,93 m) longer and providing accommodation for up to 200 passengers. This will feature modified flaps and a max take-off weight of 178,525 lb (80 980 kg). The A320 is the first subsonic commercial aircraft to have fly-by-wire control throughout normal flight.

AIRBUS A320-200

Dimensions: Span, 111 ft 3 in (33,91 m); length, 123 ft 3 in (37,58 m); height, 38 ft 8½ in (11,80 m); wing area, 1,317·5 sq ft (122,40 m²).

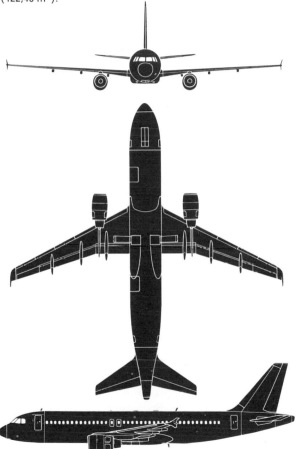

AIRTECH CN-235-100

Countries of Origin: Spain and Indonesia.

Type: Regional commercial transport and (CN-235M) military freighter.

Power Plant: Two 1,750 shp General Electric CT7-9C turbo-props.

Performance: Max cruise speed, 281 mph (452 km/h) at 15,000 ft (4 575 m); max initial climb, 1,525 ft/min (7,75 m/sec); service ceiling, 26,600 ft (8 110 m); range (at long-range cruise with max payload and 45 min reserves), 770 mls (1 240 km), (with 5,291-lb/2 400-kg payload), 2,653 mls (4 270 km).

Weights: Operational empty, 20,725 lb (9,400 kg), (CN-235M) 18,960 lb (8 600 kg); max take-off, 31,747 lb (14 400 kg), (CN-235M) 33,290 lb (15 100 kg).

Accommodation: Flight crew of two and (regional airliner) seating arrangements for up to 45 passengers four abreast, or (combi) 18 passengers and two LD-3 freight containers. (CN-235M) 53 troops or 46 paratroops.

Status: First prototype flown (in Spain) on 11 November 1983, and second (in Indonesia) on 31 December 1983. First production aircraft flown (in Spain) on 19 August 1986, and first customer delivery (Merpati Nusantara) following 15 December 1986. Military version (CN-235M) ordered by Botswana, France, Indonesia (Air Force and Navy), Panama and Saudi Arabia. Total of 123 orders (66 military and 57 commercial) by beginning of 1989.

Notes: CN-235 is manufactured jointly by CASA in Spain and IPTN in Indonesia on a 50-50 basis without component duplication. A 60/70-seat derivative, the CN-260, is currently under study, together with armed ASW and maritime patrol versions of the basic CN-235.

AIRTECH CN-235-100

Dimensions: Span, 84 ft 7¾ in (25,81 m); length, 70 ft 0½ in (21,35 m); height, 26 ft 10 in (8,18 m); wing area, 636·17 sq ft (59,10 m²).

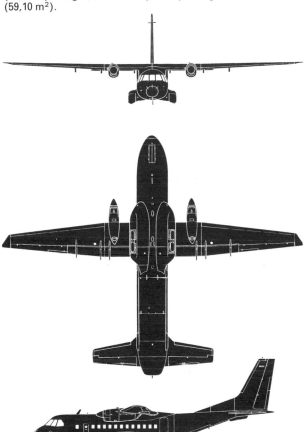

AMX INTERNATIONAL AMX

Countries of Origin: Italy and Brazil.
Type: Single-seat battlefield support and light attack aircraft.
Power Plant: One 11,030 lb st (5 000 kgp) Rolls-Royce Spey Mk 807 turbofan.
Performance: Max speed (at 23,700 lb/10 750 kg), 568 mph (913 km/h) at 36,000 ft (10 975 m), or Mach = 0·86; max initial climb, 12,600 ft/min (64 m/sec); attack radius (HI-LO-HI with 5 min combat and 10% fuel reserve), 320 mls (520 km) with 6,000 lb/2 720 kg ordnance, 550 mls (890 km) with 2,000 lb/907 kg ordnance, (LO-LO-LO), 230 mls/370 km with 6,000 lb/2 720 kg ordnance, 345 mls (555 km) with 2,000 lb/907 kg ordnance; ferry range (max external fuel and 10% reserve), 1,957 mls (3 150 km).
Weights: Operational empty, 14,770 lb (6 700 kg); max take-off, 27,557 lb (12 500 kg).
Armament: (Italian) One 20-mm rotary cannon or (Brazilian) two 30-mm cannon, two AIM-9L or similar self-defence AAMs at wingtips and max external ordnance load (including self-defence AAMs) of 8,377 lb (3 800 kg).
Status: First of seven prototypes flown (in Italy) 15 May 1984, two of these assembled in Brazil with first flying on 16 October 1985. First series aircraft flown (in Italy) on 11 May 1988. First two-seater scheduled to fly (in Italy) in June 1989. Current planning calls for 266 series single-seat (187 for Italy and 79 for Brazil) and 51 two-seat (37 for Italy and 14 for Brazil) aircraft.
Notes: The AMX has been developed jointly by Aeritalia (47·1%) and Aermacchi (23·2%) in Italy, and Embraer (29·7%) in Brazil, with three assembly lines and no component duplication. The Brazilian Air Force designation is A-1.

AMX INTERNATIONAL AMX

Dimensions: Span, 29 ft $1\frac{1}{2}$ in (8·87 m); length, 44 ft $6\frac{1}{2}$ in (13,57 m); height, 15 ft $0\frac{1}{4}$ in (4,58 m); wing area, 226·05 sq ft (21,00 m²).

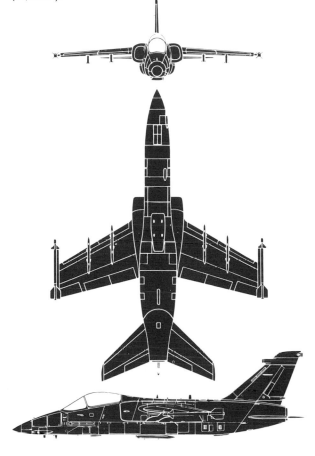

ANTONOV AN-32 (CLINE)

Country of Origin: USSR.
Type: Military tactical transport.
Power Plant: Two 4,195 ehp Ivchenko AI-20M or 5,112 ehp AI-20DM turboprops.
Performance: (AI-20DM engines) Max cruise speed, 329 mph (530 km/h) at 26,250 ft (8 000 m); econ cruise, 292 mph (470 km/h); service ceiling, 31,165 ft (9 500 m); range (no reserves and 14,770-lb/6 700-kg payload), 1,242 mls (2 000 km), no reserves and 8,157-lb/3 700-kg payload), 1,553 mls (2 500 km).
Weights: (AI-20DM engines) Empty, 37,038 lb (16 800 kg); max take-off, 59,525 lb (27 000 kg).
Accommodation: Flight crew of five and 39 troops on tip-up seats along fuselage sides, 30 fully-equipped paratroops or 24 casualty stretchers and one medical attendant.
Status: The AN-32, a derivative of the An-26 (Curl), was first flown as a prototype late 1976. Production of a version with uprated engines specifically for the Indian Air Force commenced 1982 (against initial order for 95 subsequently increased to 118) with deliveries commencing July 1984. The An-32 has also been procured by Algeria, Cape Verde, Cuba, Peru, Sao Tome and Principe, and Tanzania. The An-32 is also being supplied to the SovAF, and production in 1988 totalled 40 aircraft.
Notes: The An-32 is a growth version of the An-26 offering superior 'hot-and-high' performance. It features automatic wing leading-edge slats, triple-slotted trailing-edge flaps and a full-span fixed tailplane slot. Two racks for bombs or other stores may be attached to each side of the fuselage. The An-32 for the Indian Air Force, named Sutlej (a Punjabi river), incorporates some 15 Indian-manufactured items of avionics, including the weather radar.

ANTONOV AN-32 (CLINE)

Dimensions: Span, 95 ft 9½ in (29,20 m); length, 77 ft 8¼ in (23,68 m); height, 28 ft 8½ in (8,75 m); wing area, 807·1 sq ft (74,98 m²).

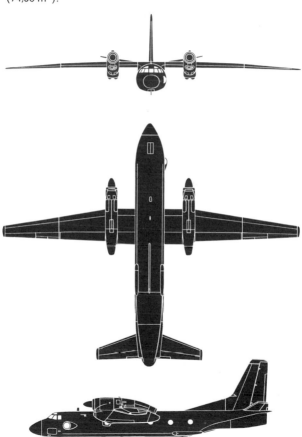

ANTONOV AN-72 & AN-74 (COALER)

Country of Origin: USSR.
Type: Light STOL transport and (An-74) arctic survey and support aircraft.
Power Plant: Two 14,330 lb st (6 500 kgp) Lotarev D-36 or (An-72A) 16,534 lb st (7 500 kgp) D-436K turbofans.
Performance: (An-72) Max speed, 438 mph (705 km/h); normal cruise, 342 mph (550 km/h) at 26,250–32,800 ft (8 000–10 000 m); range (with 22,045-lb/10 000-kg payload) 715 mls (1 150 km), (with 3,307-lb/1 500-kg payload), 2,610 mls (4 200 km); service ceiling, 32,810 ft (10 000 m).
Weights: Max take-off, 76,058 lb (34 500 kg).
Accommodation: (An-72) Flight crew of two and folding seats for 32 passengers along sidewalls or (medevac) 24 casualty stretchers and one medical attendant. (An-74) Flight crew of four (pilot, co-pilot, navigator and engineer), stations for two hydrologists and personnel cabin with four double seats and two bunks.
Status: First of two An-72 prototypes (Coaler-A) flown on 22 December 1977, with extensively revised pre-series An-72 (Coaler-C) and An-74 (Coaler-B) flying in 1985. Series production commenced 1987.
Notes: The An-72 (Coaler-C) STOL tactical transport is currently in production for and in service with the SovAF, production being scheduled to switch to the more powerful An-72A during the course of 1989. The virtually identical An-74 is a dedicated arctic survey and support version, with more advanced navaids and provision for a wheel/ski undercarriage for use in polar regions. A variant of the An-72A for airborne early warning and control tasks has been assigned the reporting name Madcap. This features a rotodome surmounting forward-swept vertical tail surfaces. Use is made of the 'Coanda effect' to achieve STOL performance, engine exhaust gases flowing over the wing upper surfaces and inboard slotted flaps.

ANTONOV AN-74 (COALER-B)

Dimensions: Span, 104 ft 7½ in (31,89 m); length, 92 ft 1¼ in (26,07 m); height, 28 ft 4½ in (8,65 m); wing area, 1,061·57 sq ft (98,62 m²).

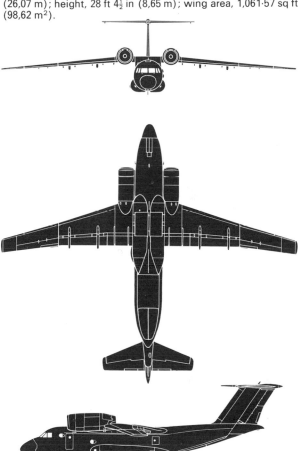

ANTONOV AN-124 RUSLAN (CONDOR)

Country of Origin: USSR.

Type: Heavy strategic freighter.

Power Plant: Four 51,590 lb st (23 400 kgp) Lotarev D-18T turbofans.

Performance: Max cruise speed, 537 mph (865 km/h); normal cruise, 497–528 mph (800–850 km/h) at 32,810–39,370 ft (10 000–12 000 m); range with 330,693-lb/150 000-kg payload), 2,795 mls (4 500 km), (with max fuel), 10,250 mls (16 500 km).

Weights: Max take-off, 892,857 lb (405 000 kg).

Accommodation: Flight crew of six and upper deck seating for relief crews and up to 88 personnel. Lower deck can accommodate all elements of the RSD-10 (SS-20 Saber) mobile intermediate-range ballistic missile system, and the largest Soviet tanks and armoured personnel carriers.

Status: First of three prototypes was flown on 26 December 1982, series production being initiated during 1984, with 15 delivered to the end of 1988, and four scheduled to be built during 1989.

Notes: The An-124 is named Ruslan after a character in Russian folklore, and, until the appearance of the An-225, was the world's largest and heaviest aircraft. Features include a fly-by-wire control system, a titanium freight hold floor and extensive use of composites. The An-124 is designed for simultaneous nose and tail loading, with a visor-type lifting nose and integral forward-folding ramp. Each main unit of the undercarriage consists of five independent twin-wheel units, permitting operation from unprepared fields, hard-packed snow and ice-covered swamp. Current low-tempo production is primarily for the SovAF, the An-124 progressively replacing the An-22. The An-124 established 21 international load-to-altitude records in July 1985, and a closed-circuit distance record in May 1987.

ANTONOV AN-124 RUSLAN (CONDOR)

Dimensions: Span, 240 ft 5¾ in (73,30 m); length, 228 ft 0¼ in (69,50 m); height, 73 ft 9¾ in (22,50 m); wing area, 6,760 sq ft (628 m²).

ANTONOV AN-225 MRIYA

Country of Origin: USSR.
Type: Ultra heavy-lift freighter.
Power Plant: Six 51,590 lb st (23 400 kgp) Lotarev D-18T turbofans.
Performance: (Manufacturer's estimates) Max cruise speed, 528 mph (850 km/h); normal cruise (with internal payload), 466 mph (750 km/h); range (with 440,917-lb/200 000 kg payload), 2,796 mls (4 500 km) at 435 mph (700 km/h).
Weights: Max take-off, 1,322,750 lb (600 000 kg).
Accommodation: Flight crew of six–eight. Freight hold of 141-ft (43-m) length can accommodate up to 551,145 lb (250 000 kg) of freight, or (externally) Buran space shuttle, a component of the Energia launch vehicle, or other outsize payload carried above fuselage.
Status: The first An-225 was flown on 21 December 1988, and a small number is expected to be built for the support of Soviet space programmes.
Notes: Evolved from the An-124 (see pages 22–23) and by far the world's largest and heaviest aircraft, the An-225 Mriya (Dream) is the result of a three-and-a-half year programme to develop a special-purpose heavy-lift transport vehicle primarily intended to carry large components of the Energia launch vehicle or the Buran space shuttle on special attachment points on top of the fuselage. For more conventional transportation tasks, the An-225 can accommodate outsize loads in its 21-ft (6,4-m) by 14·43-ft (4,4-m) cross-section freight hold. By comparison with the An-124, the An-225 has additional wing sections carrying two more turbofans, fore and aft fuselage plugs and an increased-span dihedralled tailplane with endplate fins and rudders. In addition, the number of independent twin-wheel undercarriage units has been increased to cater for the higher weights. Extensive use is made of systems thoroughly proven by the An-124, including the quadruplex fly-by-wire control system.

ANTONOV AN-225 MRIYA

Dimensions: Span, 290 ft 0 in (88,40 m); length, 275 ft 7 in (84,00 m); height, 59 ft $4\frac{1}{2}$ in (18,10 m).

ATR 72

Countries of Origin: France and Italy.
Type: Regional commercial transport.
Power Plant: Two 2,400 shp Pratt & Whitney Canada PW124 turboprops.
Performance: (Manufacturer's estimates) Max cruise speed, 326 mph (524 km/h) at 18,000 ft (5 485 m); range cruise, 285 mph (459 km/h) at 25,000 ft (7 620 m); max operating altitude, 25,000 ft (7 620 m); range (max payload and 45 min reserves), 742 mls (1 195 km), (with 66 passengers), 1,657 mls (2 666 km), (max fuel and zero payload), 2,727 mls (4 389 km).
Weights: Operational empty, 26,896 lb (12 200 kg); max take-off, 44,070 lb (19 990 kg), (optional), 47,400 lb (21 500 kg).
Accommodation: Flight crew of two and optional arrangements for 64, 66 or 70 passengers, or (high-density) 74 passengers four abreast with central aisle.
Status: Prototype ATR 72 flew 27 October 1988, with certification and first customer delivery (Finnair) scheduled for June and July 1989 respectively. Total orders placed for the ATR 72 by beginning of 1989 (including options) called for 86 aircraft. Production rate (including ATR 42) four monthly.
Notes: The ATR 72, launched in January 1986, is a stretched derivative of the ATR 42 of which 161 had been ordered (with 54 on option) by the beginning of 1989. The 100th ATR 42 was delivered in September 1988. The ATR 72 is 14 ft 9 in (4,50 m) longer than the 46–50 seat ATR 42 and is the first airliner with carbonfibre wing box, composites forming 30 per cent of the wing structure. Two versions are available with take-off weights of 19·9 and 21·5 *tonnes* respectively.

Dimensions: Span, 88 ft 9 in (27,05 m); length, 89 ft $1\frac{1}{2}$ in (27,17 m); height, 25 ft $1\frac{1}{4}$ in (7,65 m); wing area, 656·6 sq ft (61,00 m²).

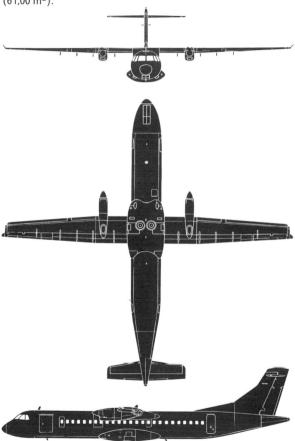

AVTEK 400A

Country of Origin: USA.
Type: Light corporate executive transport.
Power Plant: Two 680 shp Pratt & Whitney Canada PT6A-35L/R turboprops.
Performance: Max speed, 416 mph (669 km/h) at 22,000 ft (6 705 m), 389 mph (626 km/h) at 41,000 ft (12 500 m); max initial climb, 5,032 ft/min (25,6 m/sec); service ceiling, 42,500 ft (12 955 m); max range (IFR reserves), 2,396 mls (3 856 km).
Weights: Empty equipped (IFR), 3,779 lb (1 714 kg); max take-off, 6,000 lb (2 722 kg).
Accommodation: Pilot and co-pilot/passenger on flight deck and provision for up to six passengers in main cabin.
Status: First prototype flown 17 September 1984, with first of two pre-series aircraft scheduled to fly at the end of 1989, with deliveries to commence in 1990. Orders for 112 aircraft placed by beginning of 1989.
Notes: Of innovative configuration in featuring an aft-mounted swept wing with large leading-edge extensions and shoulder-mounted foreplane, the Avtek 400A is of all-composite construction. The production undercarriage has been designed by Valmet of Finland, this company having the rights to build a surveillance version, the Explorer, for the Scandinavian market. The series version differs in a number of respects from the prototype, the most noteworthy change being the introduction of sweepback on the wing to move the centre of pressure aft.

AVTEK 400A

Dimensions: Span, 34 ft 4 in (10,46 m); length, 39 ft 5 in (12,00 m); height, 10 ft 8½ in (3,26 m); wing area, 143 sq ft (13,28 m²).

BEECHCRAFT BEECHJET 400A

Country of Origin: USA (Japan).
Type: Light corporate executive transport.
Power Plant: Two 2,900 lb st (1 315 kgp) Pratt & Whitney Canada JT15D-5 turbofans.
Performance: Max speed, 530 mph (853 km/h) at 35,000 ft (10 670 m), or Mach = 0·785; typical cruise, 465 mph (748 km/h) at 39,000 ft (11 890 m); max initial climb, 3,960 ft/min (20,12 m/sec); time to 41,000 ft (12 495 m), 22 min; certified ceiling, 45,000 ft (13 715 m); range (four passengers and IFR reserves), 1,760 mls (2 832 km), (with VFR reserves), 2,220 mls (3 572 km).
Weights: Basic operational, 9,400 lb (4 264 kg); max take-off, 16,100 lb (7 303 kg).
Accommodation: Pilot and co-pilot/passenger on flight deck and optional standard arrangements for eight or nine passengers in individual seats in main cabin.
Status: Assembled at Wichita, Kansas, since 1988, the Beechjet is derived from the Mitsubishi Diamond 2, the rights to which were acquired by Beechcraft after 11 production aircraft had been built in Japan. The Model 400A, which will succeed the Model 400 currently being manufactured at 1·5–2·0 aircraft monthly, is to be certificated in December 1989, with customer deliveries commencing spring 1990.
Notes: The Beechjet 400A, total manufacturing operations for which will be undertaken at Wichita and Salina from June 1989, will differ from the Model 400 in having an increased volume interior, relocated aft fuel tankage, an improved flight deck, and increases in payload and gross take-off weight. Early in 1989, the Beechjet was to participate in a fly-off to select an off-the-shelf aircraft to fulfil the USAF's TTTS (Tanker Transport Trainer System) requirement which will involve 211 aircraft. The Beechjet was being submitted for TTTS evaluation jointly by Beechcraft and McDonnell Douglas.

BEECHCRAFT BEECHJET 400A

Dimensions: Span, 43 ft 6 in (13,25 m); length, 48 ft 5 in (14,75 m); height, 13 ft 9 in (4,19 m); wing area, 241·4 sq ft (22,43 m²).

BEECHCRAFT 2000 STARSHIP 1

Country of Origin: USA.

Type: Light corporate executive transport.

Power Plant: Two 1,200 shp Pratt & Whitney Canada PT6A-67A turboprops.

Performance: Max cruise speed, 387 mph (622 km/h); max initial climb, 3,250 ft/min (16,51 m/sec); certified ceiling, 41,000 ft (12 495 m); range (at max range power), 1,920 mls (3 090 km) with 45 min reserves.

Weights: Max take-off, 14,250 lb (6 464 kg).

Accommodation: Provision for two crew on flight deck and maximum of 10 passengers in main cabin. Six basic interior configurations offered, a typical arrangement providing seven individual seats and a two-place divan.

Status: First of three prototypes (NC-1) flown on 15 February 1986, FAA Part 23 certification being obtained on 14 June 1988. The first production aircraft (NC-4) was scheduled to be completed at the end of 1988, with the first customer delivery (NC-5) following second quarter of 1989. Production tempo of two aircraft monthly anticipated by late 1989.

Notes: Mating an aft-mounted laminar-flow wing with a variable-sweep foreplane (the sweep being changed with flap extension to provide fully-automatic pitch-trim compensation), the Starship is innovative in concept. The first certified pressurised all-composite aircraft, the Starship uses such materials as boron, carbon, Kevlar and glassfibre, and its canard configuration makes stalling impossible in landing and take-off.

BEECHCRAFT 2000 STARSHIP 1

Dimensions: Span, 54 ft 0 in (16,46 m); length, 46 ft 1 in (14,05 m); height, 12 ft 10 in (3,91 m); wing area, 280·9 sq ft (26,09 m²).

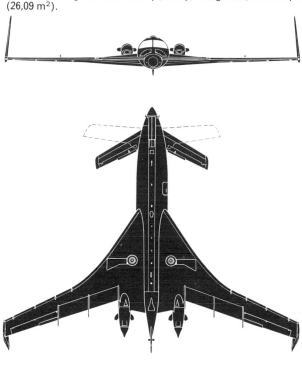

BELL/BOEING V-22 OSPREY

Country of Origin: USA.

Type: Multi-mission tilt-rotor aircraft.

Power Plant: Two 6,150 shp Allison T406-AD-400 turboshafts.

Performance: (Manufacturer's estimates) Max cruise speed (helicopter mode), 115 mph (185 km/h) at sea level, (aeroplane mode), 316 mph (509 km/h) at sea level, 345 mph (556 km/h) at optimum altitude; max forward speed with max slung load (15,000 lb/6 804 kg), 230 mph (370 km/h); range (vertical take-off with 12,000-lb/5 443-kg payload), 1,382 mls (2 224 km), (short take-off with 20,000-lb/9 072-kg payload), 2,073 mls (3 336 km); ferry range, 2,418 mls (3 892 km).

Weights: Approx empty equipped, 30,850 lb (13 993 kg); normal loaded (VTO), 47,500 lb (21 545 kg), (STO), 55,000 lb (29 947 kg); max take-off, 60,500 lb (27 442 kg).

Accommodation: Normal flight crew of three and up to 24 combat-equipped troops, 12 casualty litters plus attendants or an equivalent cargo load.

Status: First of six flying prototypes was expected to enter flight test February 1989. Current procurement plans total 657 production aircraft: 552 (MV-22A amphibious troop assault version) for US Marine Corps, 55 (CV-22A special operations support version) for the USAF, and 50 (HV-22A combat search and rescue version) for the US Navy with deliveries commencing December 1991.

Notes: Developed jointly by Bell and Boeing, the Osprey is capable of short or vertical take-offs and features a folding wing and rotor system. Production of the Osprey is scheduled to peak in 1996 at six per month and commercial versions (36–44 passengers) are under study.

BELL/BOEING V-22 OSPREY

Dimensions: Span (over rotors), 84 ft 8$\frac{4}{6}$ in (25,77 m); length (excluding probe), 62 ft 7$\frac{2}{3}$ in (19,09 m); height (over tail), 17 ft 7$\frac{3}{4}$ in (5,38 m).

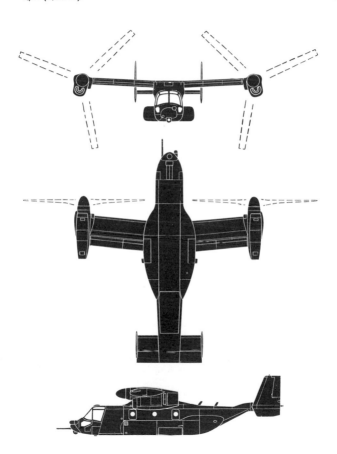

BOEING 737-500

Country of Origin: USA.
Type: Short-haul commercial transport.
Power Plant: Two 18,000 lb st (8 390 kgp) CFM International CFM 56-3-B4 or 20,000 lb st (9 070 kgp) CFM56-3-B1 turbofans.
Performance: (CFM56-3-B4) Max cruise speed (at 110,000 lb/49 900 kg), 567 mph (912 km/h) at 26,000 ft (7 925 m); long-range cruise, 494 mph (795 km/h) at 35,000 ft (10 670 m); range (with max payload), 1,565 mls (2 519 km) at 482 mph (776 km/h) at 35,000 ft (10 670 m), (with max fuel), 3,970 mls (6 389 km).
Weights: Operational empty, 68,260 lb (30 963 kg); max take-off, 115,500 lb (52 390 kg).
Accommodation: Flight crew of two with alternative cabin arrangements for 108 to 132 passengers in six abreast seating.
Status: The first Model 737-500 is scheduled to fly in June 1989, with first customer deliveries following in March 1990. Total orders for 132 -500s by beginning of 1989 (from orders for 2,264 of all Model 737 versions). One hundred and sixty-six Model 737s delivered during 1988, when production was rising from 14 monthly to 17 monthly by mid-1990.
Notes: The Model 737-500 combines the advanced technology of the -300 and -400 (see 1988 edition) with a shorter fuselage. It is offered with weights from 115,500 lb (52 390 kg) to 133,500 lb (60 550 kg). At the latter weight, with auxiliary fuel tanks and the more powerful CFM56-3-B1 engines, it will have a maximum range of 3,450 miles (5 552 km) with 108 passengers. The -500 is the latest version of the basic Model 737 which has sold in greater numbers than any other airliner. Production of the earlier -200 was completed in August 1988 with 1,114 delivered, and production is now confined to the CFM56-powered -300, -400 and -500 versions.

BOEING 737-500

Dimensions: Span, 94 ft 9 in (28,90 m); length, 101 ft 9 in (31,01 m); height, 36 ft 6 in (11,12 m); wing area, 980 sq ft (91,04 m²).

BOEING 747-400

Country of Origin: USA.

Type: Long-haul commercial transport.

Power Plant: (Options) Four 57,900 lb st (26 263 kgp) General Electric CF6-80C2, 56,750 lb st (25 742 kgp) Pratt & Whitney PW4256, or 58,000 lb st (26 309 kgp) Rolls-Royce RB.211-524D4D turbofans.

Performance: (RB.211) Max speed, 606 mph (976 km/h) at 30,000 ft (9 150 m); max cruise, 583 mph (939 km/h) at 35,000 ft (10 670 m); long-range cruise, 564 mph (907 km/h); range (max payload), 7,997 mls (12 870 km), (max fuel), 9,576 mls (15 410 km).

Weights: (RB.211) Operational empty, 393,880 lb (178 661 kg); max take-off (options), 800,000 lb (362 875 kg), 850,000 lb (385 555 kg), or 870 000 lb (394 625 kg).

Accommodation: Flight crew of two and typical three-class seating for 450 passengers, with max of 660 passengers.

Status: First Model 747-400 flown on 29 April 1988, with certification and first customer deliveries having been effected January 1989. Total of 883 Model 747s (all versions) ordered by beginning of 1989, of which 169 were -400s. Production rate of 2·5 monthly with 28 delivered during 1988.

Notes: The Model 747-400 differs in a number of respects from the -300 (see 1987 edition), the most significant external changes being an extended wing and vertical winglets. Extensive changes have been introduced in most systems, the engine nacelles have been retailored and their struts redesigned, and a new two-crew flight deck and a flight crew rest area have been introduced. By comparison with the -300, the -400 offers a 13–15 per cent reduction in fuel burn per seat, and, with increased fuel capacity and take-off weights, flights with full passenger load such as Tokyo–Paris, London–Singapore and New York-Seoul are now possible.

BOEING 747-400

Dimensions: Span, 213 ft 0 in (64,92 m); length, 231 ft $10\frac{1}{4}$ in (70,67 m); height, 63 ft 4 in (19,30 m); wing area (reference), 5,650 sq ft (524,88 m²).

BOEING 757-200

Country of Origin: USA.

Type: Short/medium-haul commercial transport.

Power Plant: (Options) Two 37,400 lb st (16 965 kgp) Rolls-Royce RB.211-535C or 40,100 lb st (18 190 kgp) RB.211-535E4, 38,200 lb st (17 327 kgp) Pratt & Whitney PW2037 or 41,700 lb st (18 915 kgp) PW2040 turbofans.

Performance: (RB.211-535E4) Max cruise speed, 570 mph (917 km/h) at 30,000 ft (9 145 m); econ cruise, 528 mph (850 km/h) at 39,000 ft (11 885 m); range (max payload), 3,660 mls (5 890 km), (max fuel), 5,257 mls (8 460 km).

Weights: Operational empty, 126,060 lb (57 180 kg); max take-off (medium range), 230,000 lb (104 325 kg), (long range), 250,000 lb (113 395 kg).

Accommodation: Flight crew of two and nine standard interior arrangements for 178 to 239 passengers. Typical arrangements include 16 first class and 170 tourist class, or 12 first class and 196 tourist class passengers.

Status: First Model 757 flown 19 February 1982, with first customer deliveries (to Eastern) December 1982 and (British Airways) January 1983. Total of 400 ordered by beginning of 1989, of which 48 delivered 1988 when production rate was four monthly.

Notes: Variants of the Model 757-200 available are the -200M Combi (illustrated above) and the -200PF (Package Freighter). The former has a mixed cargo/passenger configuration with an upward-opening cargo door in the forward fuselage port side, and the latter is a dedicated freighter with windowless interior, large side cargo door and provision for up to 15 standard (88 in/2,24 m by 125 in/3,18 m) cargo pallets on the main deck. With RB.211-535C engines, the Model 757-200 is claimed to provide 53 per cent reduction in fuel burn per seat by comparison with previous generation medium-haul airliners. A corporate executive version is available.

BOEING 757-200

Dimensions: Span, 124 ft 10 in (38,05 m); length, 155 ft 3 in (47,32 m); height, 44 ft 6 in (13,56 m); wing area, 1,994 sq ft (185,25 m²).

BOEING 767-300

Country of Origin: USA.

Type: Medium-haul commercial transport.

Power Plant: Two 52,500 lb st (23 815 kgp) General Electric CF6-80C2B2 or 50,200 lb st (22 770 kgp) Pratt & Whitney PW4050 turbofans.

Performance: (CF6-80C2B2) Max cruise speed (at 260,000 lb/ 117 935 kg), 563 mph (906 km/h) at 39,000 ft (11 890 m); long-range cruise, 529 mph (852 km/h) at 39,000 ft (11 890 m); range (max payload), 3,706 mls (5 965 km), (max fuel), 6,160 mls (9 915 km).

Weights: Operational empty, 184,000 lb (83 461 kg); max take-off, 345,000 lb (156 489 kg).

Accommodation: Normal flight crew of two (with optional third position) and max capacity of 290 passengers mainly in eight-abreast seating. Basic arrangement for 18 first class passengers in six-abreast seating and 198 tourist class passengers in mainly seven-abreast seating.

Status: First Model 767 flown on 26 September 1981, with first customer delivery (-200) on 18 August 1982. First -300 flown on 1 February 1986, with first customer delivery on 25 September 1986. Total orders (-200 and -300) by beginning of 1989 comprised 349 aircraft of which 52 delivered during 1988, when production rate was 4·5 monthly.

Notes: The -300 version of the Model 767 differs from the -200 (see 1986 edition) primarily in having a 21·25-ft (6,48 m) fuselage stretch, a strengthened undercarriage and increased gauge skinning in certain areas. An extended-range version, the -300ER, has enlarged wing centre section fuel tanks and higher gross weight. Studies have been conducted for a further stretched version, the -400, with additional fuselage plugs totalling some 10 ft (3,00 m) to provide accommodation for some 28 more passengers.

BOEING 767-300

Dimensions: Span, 156 ft 1 in (47,57 m); length, 180 ft 3 in (54,94 m); height, 52 ft 0 in (15,85 m); wing area, 3,050 sq ft (283,3 m²).

BOEING E-3 SENTRY

Country of Origin: USA.

Type: Airborne warning and control system aircraft.

Power Plant: Four 21,000 lb st (9 525 kgp) Pratt & Whitney TF33-PW-100/100A or 22,000 lb st (9 980 kgp) CFM International CFM56-2A-2 turbofans.

Performance: (TF33) Max speed, 530 mph (853 km/h); average cruise, 479 mph (771 km/h) at 28,900 ft (8 810 m); average loiter speed, 376 mph (605 km/h); time on station (unrefuelled) at 1,000 mls (1 610 km) from base, 6 hrs, (with one refuelling) 14·4 hrs; ferry range, 5,034 mls (8 100 km) at 475 mph (764 km).

Weights: (TF33) Empty, 170,277 lb (77 238 kg); normal loaded, 214,300 lb (97 206 kg); max take-off, 325,000 lb (147 420 kg).

Accommodation: Basic operational crew of 20, including flight crew of four plus 16 air defence and systems maintenance personnel (this number can vary for tactical and defence missions).

Status: First of two (EC-137D) development aircraft flown 9 February 1972, two pre-series E-3As following in 1975. The two EC-137Ds and 22 E-3As subsequently updated to E-3B standards and redelivered from July 1984, and final 10 for USAF (including updated third test aircraft) were delivered as E-3Cs. Eighteen delivered (in similar configuration to E-3C) to multi-national NATO force. Five CFM56-powered aircraft delivered to Royal Saudi Air Force. Seven CFM56-powered aircraft to be delivered to RAF (as Sentry AEW Mk 1) and four to French Air Force in 1991.

Notes: The CFM56-engined version of the E-3 (illustrated opposite) now in production for the UK and France will have flight refuelling, avionics installation being conducted in the respective countries.

BOEING E-3 SENTRY

Dimensions: Span, 145 ft 9 in (44,42 m); length, 152 ft 11 in (46,61 m); height, 41 ft 9 in (12,73 m); wing area, 2,892 sq ft (268,67 m²).

BOEING CANADA DASH 8-300

Country of Origin: Canada.
Type: Regional airliner.
Power Plant: Two 2,380 shp Pratt & Whitney Canada PW123 turboprops.
Performance: Max cruise speed (at 30,500 lb/13 834 kg), 329 mph (530 km/h) at 15,000 ft (4 575 m), 326 mph (524 km/h) at 20,000 ft (6 100 m); certificated ceiling, 25,000 ft (7 620 m); range (full passenger load), 1 025 mls (1 649 km), (with 6,000-lb/2 720-kg payload), 1,070 mls (1 723 km).
Weights: Operational empty, 24,700 lb (11 204 kg); max take-off, 41,100 lb (18 643 kg).
Accommodation: Flight crew of two and standard arrangement for 50 passengers four abreast with central aisle, and optional arrangement for 56 passengers.
Status: The Dash 8-300 prototype (converted from Dash 8-100) flown on 15 May 1987, with first customer delivery scheduled for 27 February 1989. Forty-eight orders and eight options for -300 by beginning of 1989, plus orders for 187 and options for nine -100s of which 118 delivered by end of 1988.
Notes: Manufactured by the de Havilland Division of Boeing of Canada Ltd, the Dash 8-300 embodies an 11·25-ft (3,43-m) fuselage stretch, longer-span wing, strengthened undercarriage and more powerful engines. A further stretched version under consideration at the beginning of 1989, the Dash 8-400, features a 10 ft (3·05 m) lengthening by comparison with the -300. Accommodation will be provided for 64–70 passengers. The Dash 8 is adaptable for a wide range of missions, and the -300M is proposed for the anti-submarine warfare role.

BOEING CANADA DASH 8-300

Dimensions: Span, 90 ft 0 in (27,43 m); length, 84 ft 3 in (25,68 m); height, 24 ft 7 in (7,49 m); wing area, 605 sq ft (56,21 m²).

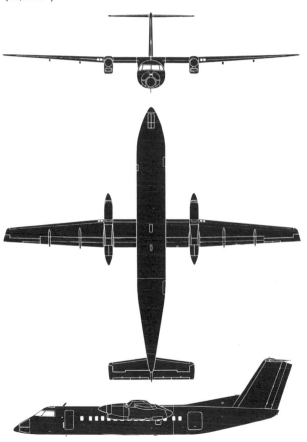

BRITISH AEROSPACE 125-800

Country of Origin: United Kingdom.
Type: Light corporate executive transport.
Power Plant: Two 4,300 lb st (1 950 kgp) Garrett TFE371-5R-1H turbofans.
Performance: Max cruise speed, 525 mph (845 km/h) at 29,000 ft (8 840 m); econ cruise, 461 mph (741 km/h) at 39,000–43,000 ft (11 900–13 100 m); max initial climb, 3,100 ft/min (15,75 m/sec); service ceiling, 43,000 ft (13 100 m); range (with max payload), 3,305 mls (5 318 km), (max fuel with VFR reserves), 3,454 mls (5 560 km).
Weights: Operational empty (typical), 15,120 lb (6 858 kg); max take-off, 27,400 lb (12 430 kg).
Accommodation: Flight crew of two with provision for third crew member, and standard arrangement for eight passengers in main cabin, with optional arrangements for up to 14 passengers.
Status: Prototype of Series 800 flown on 26 May 1983, with initial customer deliveries commencing in following year, and sales totalling 151 by beginning of 1989 of 724 (all versions) BAe 125s sold. Production continuing at rate of two monthly.
Notes: The Series 800 version of the BAe 125 is an extensively revised development of the Series 700 with more powerful engines, new, longer-span outboard wing sections, new ailerons, redesigned flight deck and larger ventral fuel tank. Six have been ordered as C-29As by the USAF for the combat flight inspection and navigation mission, and, in collaboration with Rockwell International, BAe had, at the beginning of 1989, submitted the BAe 125-800 as a contender in the USAF's TTTS (Tanker Transport Training System) contest. The Series 800A is intended specifically for the US market and the Series 800B for the rest of the world. The Series 800 is used for the aeromedical role by REGA Swiss Air Ambulance with provision for two stretchers and comprehensive intensive care equipment.

BRITISH AEROSPACE 125-800

Dimensions: Span, 51 ft 4½ in (15,66 m); length, 51 ft 2 in (15,59 m); height, 17 ft 7 in (5,37 m); wing area, 374 sq ft (32,75 m²).

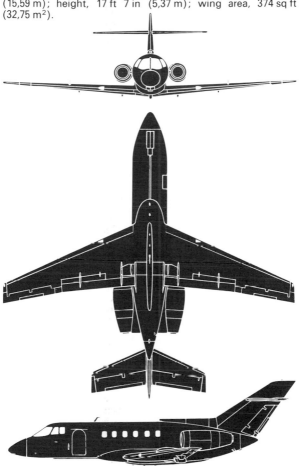

BRITISH AEROSPACE 146-300

Country of Origin: United Kingdom.
Type: Short-haul regional airliner.
Power Plant: Four 6,970 lb st (3 161 kgp) Textron Lycoming ALF502R-5 turbofans.
Performance: Max cruise, 487 mpg (784 km/h) at 24,000 ft (7 315 m); econ cruise, 439 mph (706 km/h) at 31,000 ft (9 450 m); range (max payload of 23,500 lb/10 660 kg), 1,588 mls (2 556 km), (optional fuel and 18,446-lb/8 367-kg payload), 2,154 mls (3 467 km).
Weights: Operational empty (typical), 54,000 lb (24,494 kg); max take-off, 95,000 lb (43 092 kg).
Accommodation: Flight crew of two and 100 passengers five abreast or 112 passengers six abreast in high-density seating. Various mixed-class options available (eg, 35 business and 65 economy class, or 10 first class and 84 economy class).
Status: Aerodynamic prototype of 146-300 (conversion of first 146 Srs 100 prototype) flown on 1 May 1987 with certification in September 1988. First customer delivery of 146-300 (to United Express) last quarter of 1988. Production rate of all versions rising from 2·0 to 3·3 monthly at beginning of 1989 when firm orders totalled 150 aircraft with 114 delivered.
Notes: The -100 and -200 series 146 differ from the -300 described and illustrated essentially in fuselage length, these being respectively 86 ft 5 in (26,34 m) and 93 ft 10 in (28,6 m). The 146-200 is available in QT (Quiet Trader) dedicated freighter form with strengthened floor and freight door as is also the 146-300, both being ordered by TNT Aviation, and in an executive version known as the Statesman.

BRITISH AEROSPACE 146-300

Dimensions: Span, 86 ft 5 in (26,34 m); length, 101 ft 8 in (30,99 m); height, 28 ft 3 in (8,61 m); wing area, 832 sq ft (77,30 m²).

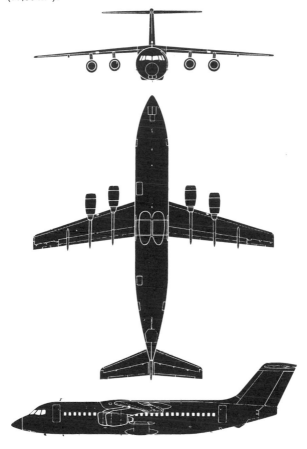

BRITISH AEROSPACE 146STA

Country of Origin: United Kingdom.
Type: Military tactical transport.
Power Plant: Four 6,970 lb st (3 161 kgp) Textron Lycoming ALF502R-MR turbofans.
Performance: Max cruise, 489 mph (788 km/h) at 24,000 ft (7 315 m); tactical radius (with 60 fully-equipped paratroops, HI-LO-HI mission profile), 932 mls (1 500 km) including 58 mls (93 km) at 500 ft (152 m) on each side of DZ: range (with max freight payload of 22,750 lb/10 319 kg), 1,370 mls (2 205 km).
Weights: Operational empty (non-palletised freight), 48,650 lb (22 068 kg), (palletised freight), 53,250 lb (24 154 kg); max take-off, 93,000 lb (42 185 kg).
Accommodation: Sixty fully-equipped paratroops in paratroop seats, 80 personnel in airline-standard seating, or (typical for casevac) 18 casualty stretchers, 26 seated wounded and four medical attendants. As a freighter five standard 108 in by 88 in (2,74 m by 2,24 m) pallets each loaded up to 4,000 lb (1 815 kg) may be carried.
Status: The prototype 146STA (conversion of second 146 Srs 100 prototype) was flown on 8 August 1988.
Notes: The 146STA (Sideloading Tactical Airlifter) is the first dedicated military variant of the 146 commercial transport. The sideloading freight door is identical with that of the commercial 146-200QT Quiet Trader and an integral ramp system has been introduced to facilitate loading and unloading of wheeled equipment or vehicles. On each side of the hold aft of the main cargo door an air-openable parachuting door may be installed, together with an air delivery system for re-supply missions. Flight refuelling equipment is an option, and potential roles include those of two-point air-air refuelling tanker and search and rescue, the latter mission involving installation of a dual-mode (weather and surveillance) radar.

BRITISH AEROSPACE 146STA

Dimensions: Span, 86 ft 5 in (26,34 m); length, 85 ft 11 in (26,19 m); height, 28 ft 3 in (8,61 m); wing area, 832 sq ft (77,30 m²).

BRITISH AEROSPACE ATP

Country of Origin: United Kingdom.
Type: Regional commercial transport.
Power Plant: Two 2,400 shp Pratt & Whitney PW124A or 2,653 shp PW126 turboprops.
Performance: Max cruise speed, 306 mph (485 km/h) at 15,000 ft (4 670 m); econ cruise, 301 mph (485 km/h) at 18,000 ft (5 485 m); typical initial climb, 1,370 ft/min (6,96 m/sec); range (with max payload of 14,830 lb/6 727 kg), 980 mls (1 577 km) at econ cruise, (with 8,330-lb/3 778-kg payload), 2,725 mls (4 386 km).
Weights: Operational empty (typical), 29,970 lb (13 594 kg); max take-off, 49,500 lb (22 453 kg).
Accommodation: Flight crew of two and standard arrangement for 64 passengers four abreast, with optional high-density arrangement for 72 passengers.
Status: Two prototypes flown on 6 August 1986 and 20 February 1987, with certification following in March 1988. The first customer delivery (to British Midland) was made in April 1988, and deliveries and firm orders totalled 26 aircraft by the beginning of 1989, when production commitments totalled 45 ATPs and production was running at one aircraft monthly.
Notes: Claimed to be the only new-generation turboprop airliner capable of utilising jetways at major airports, the ATP (Advanced Turboprop) is technically a stretched development of the 748, with new engines, systems and equipment, swept vertical surfaces and redesigned fuselage nose. It also incorporates an advanced flight deck with EFIS (Electronic Flight Instrument System). A maritime surveillance version of the ATP with search radar, magnetic anomaly detector and weapons hardpoints has been proposed.

BRITISH AEROSPACE ATP

Dimensions: Span, 100 ft 6 in (30,63 m); length, 85 ft 4 in (26,01 m); height, 23 ft 5 in (7,14 m); wing area, 842·84 sq ft (78,30 m²).

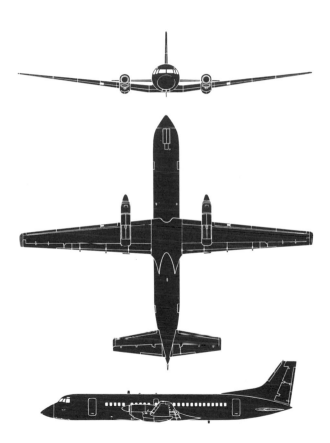

BRITISH AEROSPACE HARRIER GR MK 5

Countries of Origin: United Kingdom and USA.
Type: Single-seat V/STOL close support and tactical reconnaissance aircraft.
Power Plant: One 21,750 lb st (9 866 kgp) Rolls-Royce Pegasus Mk 105 vectored-thrust turbofan.
Performance: Max speed, 661 mph (1 065 km/h) at sea level, or Mach = 0·87, 600 mph (966 km/h) at 36,000 ft (10 975 m), or Mach = 0·91; tactical radius (with 12 Mk 82 bombs and one hour loiter), 103 mls (167 km), (HI-LO-HI mission profile with two 250 Imp gal/1 136 l external tanks and seven Mk 82 bombs, but no allowance for loiter), 553 mls (889 km); ferry range (with four 250 Imp gal/1 136 l tanks retained), 2,015 mls (3 243 km).
Weights: Operational empty (including pilot), 13,984 lb (6 343 kg); max take-off (VTO), 18,950 lb (8 595 kg), (STO) 31,000 lb (14 061 kg).
Armament: Two 25-mm cannon (on under-fuselage stations) and up to 16 Mk 82 or six Mk 83 bombs, six BL-755 cluster bombs, four Maverick ASMs, or 10 rocket pods on six wing stations. Max external load, 9,200 lb (4 173 kg).
Status: First of two weapon system development aircraft flown on 30 April 1985, with formal acceptance by the RAF against initial order for 60 series aircraft taking place on 30 March 1988. Contract for further 34 announced 19 April 1988.
Notes: The Harrier GR Mk 5 is the RAF equivalent of the US Marine Corps' AV-8B. Aircraft built against second contract (34 aircraft) expected to be completed to upgraded GR Mk 7 standard to which first 41 will be retrofitted. Final 19 of first contract to be completed to an interim standard.

BRITISH AEROSPACE HARRIER GR MK 5

Dimensions: Span, 30 ft 4 in (9,24 m); length, 46 ft 4 in (14,12 m); height, 11 ft 7¾ in (3,55 m); wing area (including LERX), 238·7 sq ft (22,18 m²).

BRITISH AEROSPACE HAWK 100

Country of Origin: United Kingdom.
Type: Tandem two-seat advanced systems trainer and (single-seat) light multi-role attack aircraft.
Power Plant: One 5,845 lb st (2 650 kgp) Rolls-Royce Turboméca Adour 871 turbofan.
Performance: Max speed, 644 mph (1 037 km/h) at sea level, or Mach = 0·845; econ cruise, 495 mph (796 km/h) at 41,000 ft (12 500 m); combat radius (light strike with HI-LO-HI mission profile), 759 mls (1 222 km) with 1,000-lb (453,6-kg) bombs, 316 mls (509 km) with seven 1,000-lb (453,6-kg) bombs; endurance (combat air patrol with two Sidewinder-type AAMs and one 30-mm cannon), 3·5 hrs on station 160 mls (260 km) from base.
Weights: Empty, 8,500 lb (3 855 kg); max take-off, 18,890 lb (8 570 kg).
Armament: Max external ordnance load (when flown as single-seater) of 7,200 lb (3 265 kg).
Status: Aerodynamic prototype of Hawk 100 (modified from manufacturer's Hawk 60 demonstrator) flown on 1 October 1987, and deliveries to launch customer (Royal Saudi Air Force) to commence 1990–91.
Notes: An enhanced development of the Hawk basic/advanced trainer (see 1985 edition), the Hawk 100 will have an inertial navigation system, head-up display, and (optional) laser ranging and forward-looking infrared.

BRITISH AEROSPACE HAWK 100

Dimensions: Span, 30 ft 9¾ in (9,39 m); length (excluding probe), 38 ft 4 in (11,68 m); height, 13 ft 8 in (4,15 m); wing area, 179·64 sq ft (16,69 m²).

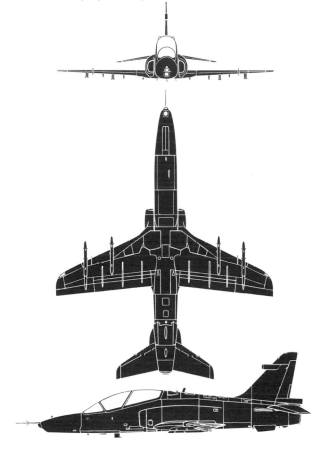

BRITISH AEROSPACE HAWK 200

Country of Origin: United Kingdom.
Type: Single-seat multi-role lightweight fighter.
Power Plant: One 5,845 lb st (2 650 kgp) Rolls-Royce Turboméca Adour 871 turbofan.
Performance: Max speed, 645 mph (1 037 km/h) at 8,000 ft (2 440 m), or Mach=0·87; max cruise, 633 mph (1 019 km/h) at sea level; econ cruise, 495 mph (796 km/h) at 41,000 ft (12 500 m); max initial climb, 11,510 ft/min (58,47 m/sec); service ceiling, 50,000 ft (15 250 m); range (internal fuel), 554 mls (892 km), (with max external fuel), 2,244 mls (3 610 km); tactical radius (HI-LO-LO-HI with two 130 Imp gal/592 l drop tanks and three Sea Eagle ASMs), 383 mls (617 km).
Weights: Empty, 9,100 lb (4 127 kg); max take-off, 20,065 lb (9 101 kg).
Armament: One or two internal 25-mm or 27-mm cannon. Maximum ordnance (including cannon) of 7,700 lb (3 500 kg) with centreline and four wing stores stations.
Status: First prototype flown on 19 May 1986, with first pre-production aircraft following on 24 April 1987. Initial deliveries to launch customer (Royal Saudi Air Force) expected 1990–91.
Notes: A dedicated single-seat multi-role lightweight combat derivative of the two-seat Hawk basic/advanced trainer and tactical aircraft, sharing with the Hawk 100 (see pages 58–59) the Adour 871 engine and much of the avionic equipment, the Hawk 200 has been developed as a private venture. The preponderance of the 60 Hawks included in the Project *Al Yamamah* 2—the second phase in an equipment programme for the Royal Saudi Air Force—announced on 3 July 1988 are understood to be of this version. The Hawk 200 retains 80 per cent structural commonality aft of the cockpit with the current production two-seat versions.

Dimensions: Span, 30 ft 9¾ in (9,39 m); length, 37 ft 4 in (11,38 m); height, 13 ft 8 in (4,15 m); wing area, 179·64 sq ft (16,69 m²).

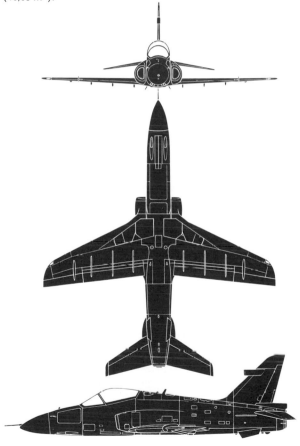

BRITISH AEROSPACE JETSTREAM SUPER 31

Country of Origin: United Kingdom.

Type: Light regional airliner and corporate transport.

Power Plant: Two 1,020 shp Garrett TPE331-12 turboprops.

Performance: Max cruise speed, 303 mph (488 km/h) at 15,000 ft (4 570 m); econ cruise, 267 mph (430 km/h) at 25,000 ft (7 620 m); max initial climb, 2,100 ft/min (10,67 m/sec); range (IFR reserves and 19 passengers), 805 mls (1 296 km), (18 passengers, flight attendant and galley), 690 mls (1 111 km).

Weights: Operational empty, 9,733 lb (4 415 kg); max take-off, 16,204 lb (7 350 kg).

Accommodation: Flight crew of two and commuter airliner arrangements for 18–19 passengers three abreast, or basic corporate executive seating for eight passengers and optional 12-seat executive shuttle arrangement.

Status: The Jetstream Super 31 replaced the Jetstream 31 from September 1988, customer deliveries commencing in that month (to Northwest Airlink). First Jetstream 31 was flown 18 March 1982, and orders for both 31s and Super 31s totalled 237 by the beginning of 1989, with some 205 delivered and production continuing at four aircraft monthly.

Notes: The Super 31 differs from the preceding Jetstream 31 primarily in having uprated engines, a simplified wing structure, an improved cabin and an increase in maximum take-off weight. At the beginning of 1989, BAe was proposing a stretched 29-seat development, the Jetstream 41, with an all-up weight nearly 6,000 lb (2 722 kg) more than the Super 31 at 22,046 lb (10 000 kg). The fuselage is to be raised in relation to the wing which will span 60 ft 0 in (18,29 m), and overall length will be 63 ft 2 in (19,25 m). Power plant had not been finalised, but consideration was being given to the 1,500 shp (flat rated) Garrett TPE331-14.

BRITISH AEROSPACE JETSTREAM SUPER 31

Dimensions: Span, 52 ft 0 in (15,85 m); length, 47 ft 2 in (14,37 m); height, 17 ft 6 in (5,37 m); wing area, 270 sq ft (25,08 m²).

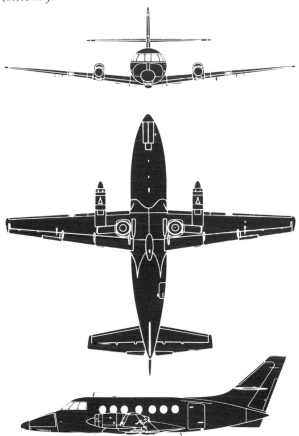

BRITISH AEROSPACE SEA HARRIER FRS MK 2

Country of Origin: United Kingdom.
Type: Single-seat V/STOL shipboard multi-role fighter.
Power Plant: One 21,500 lb st (9 760 kgp) Rolls-Royce Pegasus 104 vectored-thrust turbofan.
Performance: Max speed, 720 mph (1 160 km/h) at 1,000 ft (305 m), or Mach=0.95, 607 mph (977 km/h) at 36,000 ft (10 975 m), or Mach=0.92, (with two each Martel ASMs and AIM-9L AAMs), 598 mph (962 km/h) at sea level, or Mach= 0.83; combat radius (high-altitude intercept with 3 min combat), 480 mls (750 km/h), (surface attack with two Sea Eagle AShMs and two 30-mm cannon), 230 mls (370 km).
Weights: Approx operational empty, 14,500 lb (6 577 kg); max take-off, 26,500 lb (12 020 kg).
Armament: External fuselage packs for two 25-mm or 30-mm cannon, or two AIM-20 AAM pylons on fuselage stations, plus two stores stations under each wing for free-fall or retarded 1,000-lb (453,6-kg) bombs, cluster bombs, Matra 115/116 68-mm rocket packs, AIM-9L or AIM-120 AAMs, Sea Eagle AShMs, or ALARM anti-radiation missiles.
Status: The first of two development FRS Mk 2s was flown 19 September 1988. Some 40 FRS MK 1s to be rotated through midlife update programme to FRS Mk 2 standard 1991–94, with initial operational service scheduled for 1992.
Notes: Essentially an upgrade of the Sea Harrier FRS Mk 1, the FRS MK 2 differs in having a Blue Vixen pulse-Doppler radar providing 'look-down/shootdown' capability and the ability to carry up to four AIM-120 air-air missiles. It also embodies a 1 ft $1\frac{3}{4}$ in (35 cm) aft fuselage lengthening, a redesigned cockpit and improved systems. A total of 57 FRS Mk 1s were supplied to the Royal Navy, and 23 similar Mk 51s to the Indian Navy.

BRITISH AEROSPACE SEA HARRIER FRS MK 2

Dimensions: Span, 27 ft 3 in (8,31 m); length, 46 ft 3 in (14,10 m); height, 12 ft 2 in (3,71 m).

BROMON BR-2000

Country of Origin: USA.
Type: Light utility military and commercial transport.
Power Plant: Two 1,750 shp General Electric CT7-9B turbo-props.
Performance: (Manufacturer's estimates) Max cruise speed, 258 mph (415 km/h); normal cruise, 242 mph (389 km/h); max initial climb, 1,790 ft/min (9,1 m/sec); service ceiling, 25,000 ft (7 620 m); range (with 10,000-lb/4 536-kg payload), 1,150 mls (1 850 km), (with max fuel and 5,855-lb/2 656-kg payload), 2,418 mls (3 890 km); ferry range, 2,650 mls (4 265 km).
Weights: Empty, 15,000 lb (6 804 kg); max take-off, 31,500 lb (14 288 kg).
Accommodation: Flight crew of two and up to 46 passengers four abreast with central aisle, or (military transport), max of 50 personnel, 35 combat-equipped troops or three 463L standard military pallets. Maximum payload, 13,705 lb (6 217 kg).
Status: First of five prototypes scheduled to enter flight test in July 1989, with certification programme completed in July 1990. A letter of intent for 15 aircraft received from Philippine Air Force, and negotiations for joint-venture licensing in Taiwan being conducted late 1988.
Notes: The BR-2000 is an unpressurised aircraft of fundamentally simply design and of largely conventional metal construction. To possess short take-off and landing characteristics, it is designed specifically for rough-field operation with minimal maintenance facilities in the undeveloped areas of the world. The BR-2000 is intended as a multi-mission aircraft for both civil and military use, its envisaged roles including border patrol, forestry surveillance and medevac, up to 36 casualty stretchers being accommodated for the last-mentioned mission. Provision is being made for three hardpoints on each wing for external stores.

BROMON BR-2000

Dimensions: Span, 82 ft 4 in (25,09 m); length, 77 ft 1 in (23,49 m); height, 27 ft 8 in (8,43 m).

CANADAIR CHALLENGER 601-3A

Country of Origin: Canada.

Type: Light corporate executive transport.

Power Plant: Two 9,140 lb st (4 146 kgp) General Electric CF34-3A turbofans.

Performance: Max cruise speed, 529 mph (815 km/h) at 36,000 ft (10 975 m), or Mach = 0·8; normal cruise, 509 mph (819 km/h); long-range cruise, 488 mph (786 km/h); operational ceiling, 41,000 ft (12 500 m); range (max fuel, five passengers and IFR reserves), 3,950 mls (6 356 km), (long-range option from first quarter 1989), 4,142 mls (6 667 km).

Weights: Manufacturer's empty, 20,485 lb (9 292 kg); operational empty (typical), 24,685 lb (11 197 kg); max take-off, 43,100 lb (19 550 kg); (long-range option), operational empty, 24,885 lb (11 288 kg); max take-off, 44,600 lb (20 230 kg).

Accommodation: Flight crew of two with customer-specified main cabin arrangement for up to 19 passengers.

Status: Prototype Challenger 601 flown on 10 April 1982, and first 601-3A on 28 September 1986, with 35 of latter delivered by beginning of 1989 (of 184 Challengers of all versions) when production rate was two aircraft monthly.

Notes: The 601-3A is the current production version of the Challenger, this being the intercontinental-range derivative of the transcontinental Challenger 600. At the beginning of 1989, design had been frozen of the Canadair RJ (Regional Jet) derivative of the Challenger 601 configured for 48–52 passengers. With similar engines to the 601-3A, the RJ will feature a 70 ft 4 in (21,44 m) fuselage.

CANADAIR CHALLENGER 601-3A

Dimensions: Span, 64 ft 4 in (19,61 m); length, 68 ft 5 in (20,85 m); height, 20 ft 8 in (6,30 m); wing area, 450 sq ft (41,82 m²).

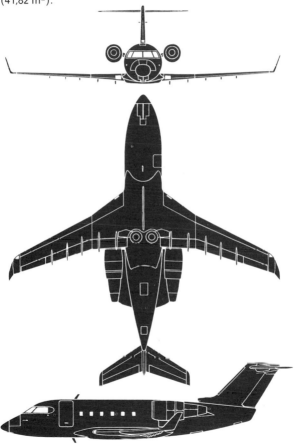

CANADAIR CL-215T

Country of Origin: Canada.

Type: Multi-purpose amphibian.

Power Plant: Two 2,380 shp Pratt & Whitney Canada PW123AF turboprops.

Performance: (Manufacturer's estimates) Max cruise speed (at 35,000 lb/15 876 kg), 227 mph (365 km/h) at 5,000 ft (1 525 m); normal cruise (75% power), 214 mph (345 km/h); range cruise, 199 mph (320 km/h) at 5,000 ft (1 525 m), 201 mph (324 km/h) at 10,000 ft (3 050 m); max initial climb (at 46,000 lb/ 20 865 kg), 1,220 ft/min (6,2 m/sec); ferry range, 1,295 mls (2 085 km).

Weights: Operational empty (typical utility), 24,600 lb (11 158 kg); max take-off (utility from water), 37,700 lb (17 100 kg), (from land), 43,850 lb (19 890 kg).

Accommodation: Normal flight crew of two with additional stations for flight engineer, navigator and two observers for maritime surveillance, or 32–35 passengers in transport configuration. Maximum disposable payload (water bomber) of 13,500 lb (6 123 kg) or (utility) 10,560 lb (4 790 kg).

Status: First of two prototypes scheduled to fly early 1989 with certification in following autumn, these being last two of 111 airframes laid down as piston-engined CL-215s. First retrofit deliveries commencing autumn 1989, with first new-build aircraft following early 1990.

Notes: New production CL-215Ts will have powered controls and (in water bomber version) new four-door, four-tank water drop system and increased water capacity.

CANADAIR CL-215T

Dimensions: Span, 93 ft 10 in (28,60 m); length, 65 ft $0\frac{1}{4}$ in (19,82 m); height (on land), 29 ft $5\frac{1}{2}$ in (8,98 m); wing area, 1,080 sq ft (100,33 m²).

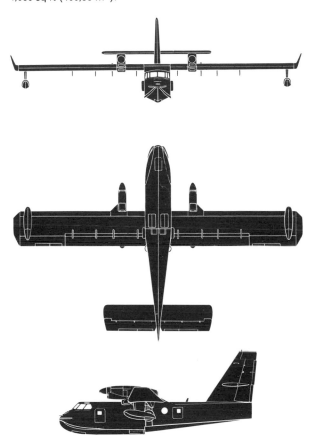

CESSNA U-27A

Country of Origin: USA.

Type: Light military utility and special missions aircraft.

Power Plant: One 600 shp Pratt & Whitney Canada PT6A-114 turboprop.

Performance: Max cruise speed, 212 mph (341 km/h) at 10,000 ft (3 050 m); max initial climb, 1,050 ft/min (5,33 m/sec); service ceiling (at 7,800 lb/3 538 kg), 25,500 ft (7 770 m); range (with reserves), 1,250 mls (2 010 km).

Weights: Standard empty, 3,862 lb (1 752 kg); max take-off, 8,000 lb (3 629 kg).

Accommodation: Flight crew of two and 14 passengers three abreast, 12 paratroops or four casualty stretchers and a medical attendant.

Status: The U-27A is a military derivative of the Cessna 208A Caravan I, an engineering prototype of which was flown on 9 December 1982, with customer deliveries commencing in February 1985. The U-27A was introduced in 1986, and three examples had been built by the beginning of 1989, by which time some 300 of the civil Caravan I had been delivered (including 199 for Federal Express) and production was continuing at a rate of 7–8 monthly.

Notes: The U-27A can be based on either the Model 208A or lengthened 208B (see 1987 edition) and has a maximum useful load of 4,173 lb (1 893 kg). Intended for troop transportation, medevac, cargo, surveillance and forward air control tasks, the U-27A can be fitted with six wing stores stations for a variety of stores, including gun pods and rockets, and is normally fitted with the 84 cu ft (2,83 m³) cargo pannier of the Models 208A and B. This pannier can be replaced by a reconnaissance pod accommodating three high-resolution day/night sensors (film or electro-optical), a video management processor, imagery recorders and data link.

CESSNA U-27A

Dimensions: Span, 52 ft 1 in (15,87 m); length, 37 ft 7 in (11,45 m); height, 14 ft 10 in (4,52 m); wing area, 279·4 sq ft (25,96 m²).

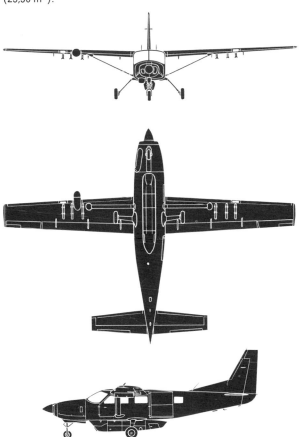

CESSNA MODEL 560 CITATION 5

Country of Origin: USA.
Type: Light corporate executive transport.
Power Plant: Two 2,900 lb st (1 315 kgp) Pratt & Whitney (Canada) JT15D-5A turbofans.
Performance: Max cruise speed (at 13,000 lb/5 897 kgp), 492 mph (791 km/h) at 33,000 ft (10 060 m), 443 mph (713 km/h) at 45,000 ft (13 715 m); max initial climb, 3,650 ft/min (18,54 m/sec); time to 35,000 ft (10 670 m), 15 min, to 43,000 ft (14 105 m), 29 min; range (six passengers and 45 min reserves), 2,211 mls (3 558 km).
Weights: Empty, 8,899 lb (4 036 kg); max take-off, 15,900 lb (7 212 kg).
Accommodation: Flight crew of two and standard seating arrangement in main cabin for seven passengers (four forward and three aft-facing individual seats).
Status: Prototype Citation 5 flown on 18 August 1987, with a pre-production prototype following in January 1988. FAA certification was obtained on 9 December 1988, with initial customer deliveries to commence in March 1989, and 34 to be built during course of year.
Notes: The latest in the Citation series of corporate executive transports to attain production, the Citation 5 is expected to supplant the earlier Citation S/II as an intermediate aircraft between the Citation II and III. It differs from its predecessor primarily in having 16 per cent more power, a 20-in (51-cm) fuselage stretch and 25 per cent more horizontal tail surface area. The JT15D-5A engines are the same as those employed by the 15 Citation S/II derivatives supplied to the US Navy as T-47A trainers.

74

CESSNA MODEL 560 CITATION 5

Dimensions: Span, 52 ft 3⅔ in (15,90 m); length, 48 ft 10⅘ in (14,90 m); height, 15 ft 0 in (4,57 m); wing area, 342·6 sq ft (31,70 m²).

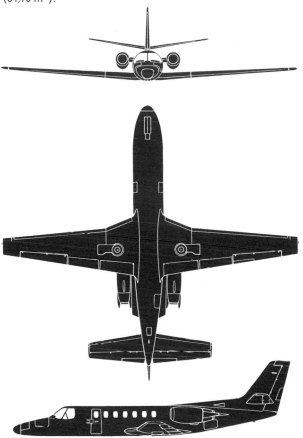

CHENGDU (CAC) F-7P SKYBOLT

Country of Origin: China (USSR).
Type: Single-seat air superiority and tactical fighter.
Power Plant: One 9,700 lb st (4 400 kgp) dry and 13,448 lb st (6 100 kgp) reheat Chengdu WP-7BM turbojet.
Performance: Max speed, 1,350 mph (2 175 km/h) above 36,090 ft (11 000 m), or Mach = 2·05; max initial climb, 35,435 ft/min (180 m/sec); service ceiling, 59,710 ft (18 200 m); range (internal fuel and two PL-2 or AIM-9 AAMs), 745 mls (1 200 km), (two AAMs and max external fuel), 1,080 mls (1 740 km).
Weights: Empty, 11,629 lb (5 275 kg); normal max take-off, 16,603 lb (7 531 kg).
Armament: Two 30-mm cannon and four PL-2, PL-7 or AIM-9 AAMs, or four 18-round 57-mm rocket pods, or two 550-lb (250-kg) and two 330-lb (150-kg) bombs.
Status: The F-7P is a modified version of the F-7M Airguard (see 1987 edition) which, in turn, was a progressive development of the F-7, a reverse-engineered version of the late 'fifties Soviet MiG-21F clear-weather air superiority fighter.
Notes: The F-7P Skybolt, an initial Pakistan Air Force order for 20 of which was fulfilled in August 1988, differs from the F-7M essentially in having provision for four AAMs. The single-seat F-7M and -7P series fighters are the responsibility of CAC (Chengdu Aircraft Company). A two-seat training version, the FT-7 (see 1988 edition) is being produced by GAIGC (Guizhou Aviation Industry Group).

CHENGDU (CAC) F-7P SKYBOLT

Dimensions: Span, 23 ft $5\frac{5}{8}$ in (7,15 m); length (excluding probe), 45 ft 9 in (13,94 m); height, 13 ft $5\frac{1}{2}$ in (4,10 m); wing area, 247·6 sq ft (23,00 m^2).

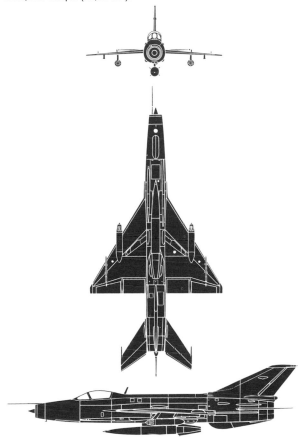

CLAUDIUS DORNIER SEASTAR

Country of Origin: Federal Germany.
Type: Light utility amphibian.
Power Plant: Two 650 shp Pratt & Whitney Canada PT6A-135A turboprops.
Performance: Max cruise speed, 219 mph (352 km/h) at 9,840 ft (3 000 m); max initial climb, 1,800 ft/min (8,0 m/sec); service ceiling, 28,000 ft (8 600 m); range (12 passengers and 10 per cent reserves), 345 mls (555 km), (with 1,000-lb/450-kg payload), 1 044 mls (1 680 km); ferry range, 1,150 mls (1 850 km).
Weights: Empty equipped, 6,181 lb (2 800 kg); max take-off, 10,154 lb (4 600 kg).
Accommodation: Pilot and co-pilot/passenger on flight deck and 12 passengers three abreast with offset aisle in main cabin (optional toilet replaces three seats). Medevac mission with provision for five stretcher cases and two medical attendants.
Status: First prototype (VT-01 flown 17 August 1984, with first of two series prototypes (CD2) following on 24 April 1987. Series production to commence during 1989, with certification late 1989 and first customer deliveries commencing summer 1990.
Notes: Of all-composite construction and intended for a wide variety of roles, including maritime surveillance, search and rescue, air ambulance and corporate transportation, the Seastar is suitable for operation from grass, water, ice and snow surfaces.

CLAUDIUS DORNIER SEASTAR

Dimensions: Span, 58 ft 4⅓ in (17,80 m); length, 40 ft 10½ in (12,46 m); height (on wheels), 15 ft 1 in (4,60 m); wing area, 329·39 sq ft (30,60 m²).

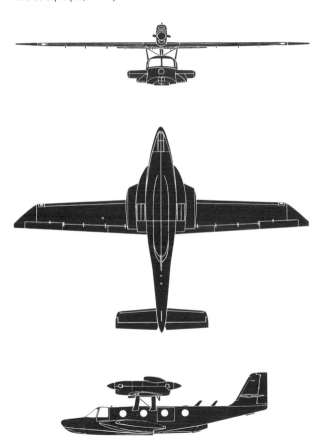

CNAMC A-5K KONG YUN (FANTAN)

Country of Origin: China.
Type: Single-seat close air support and ground attack aircraft.
Power Plant: Two 6,614 lb st (3 000 kgp) dry and 8,267 lb st (3 750 kgp) reheat Shenyang Wopen-6A turbojets.
Performance: Max speed, 752 mph (1 210 km/h) at 36,000 ft (10 975 m), or Mach = 1·2, 761 mph (1 225 km/h) at sea level, or Mach = 1·0; combat radius (with 4,410-lb/2 000-kg external stores and 10 per cent reserves), 248 mls (400 km) LO-LO-LO, 373 mls (600 km) HI-LO-HI; range (max external fuel), 1,243 mls (2 000 km); ceiling, 52,495 ft (16 000 m).
Weights: Empty, 14,625 lb (6 634 kg); max take-off, 26,455 lb (12 000 kg).
Armament: Two 23-mm Type 2H cannon plus up to 4,410 lb (2 000 kg) of ordnance distributed between two fuselage and six wing stations.
Status: First of two prototypes of the A-5K (adapted from Qiang-5 IIIs) flown on 7 September 1988.
Notes: The A-5K is one of two parallel upgrade programmes of the Qiang-5 III (A-5C), the other being the A-5M. The A-5K is an upgrade of the systems of the Qiang-5 III conducted by the French Thomson-CSF concern, whereas the A-5M is an upgrade performed by Aeritalia but incorporating similar systems to those of the Italo-Brazilian AMX. The A-5K has a nav/attack system including a Thomson-CSF head-up display and laser ranger, a SAGEM Uliss 90 inertial navigation system, a TRT radio altimeter, an Omera camera and instrumentation provided by SFIM and SFENA. Like the A-5M, the A-5K has uprated Wopen-6A engines. Both the A-5K and A-5M upgrades are theoretically intended primarily for export aircraft (both newbuild and existing—some 150 A-5s having been supplied to Pakistan and North Korea), but could be applicable to the 500 or so aircraft serving with the People's Republic of China Air Force.

CNAMC A-5K KONG YUN (FANTAN)

Dimensions: Span, 31 ft 10 in (9,70 m); length (excluding probe) 50 ft $6\frac{7}{8}$ in (15,41 m); height, 14 ft $9\frac{1}{2}$ in (4,51 m); wing area, 300·85 sq ft (27,95 m²).

CONAIR TURBO FIRECAT

Country of Origin: Canada (USA).
Type: Fire-fighting aircraft.
Power Plant: Two 1,424 shp Pratt & Whitney (Canada) PT6-67AF turboprops.
Performance: Max cruise speed (at 26,000 lb/11 793 kg), 253 mph (408 km/h); normal drop speed, 138 mph (222 km/h); endurance (with max payload), 5·1 hrs.
Weights: Operational empty, 13,600 lb (6 169 kg); max take-off, 26,000 lb (11 793 kg).
Accommodation: Minimum crew of one pilot.
Status: First conversion (from piston-engined Firecat) flown on 7 August 1988, current planning calling for conversion to similar standards of the entire 14-aircraft Firecat fleet of France's *Securité Civile* during 1988–91, as well as Conair's own 11-aircraft fleet.
Notes: The Turbo Firecat is a conversion by Conair of the Firecat, itself a conversion of the Grumman S-2 Tracker anti-submarine warfare aircraft, developed in co-operation with the IMP Group. Like the Firecat, the Turbo Firecat is a dedicated fire-fighting aircraft with a 863-Imp gal (3 295-l) fire retardant delivery tank, single-point underwing refuelling, two 83-Imp gal (379-l) underwing tanks and a 38-Imp gal (173-l) foam injection system. A similarly re-engined conversion of the ASW CP-121 Tracker (loaned from the Canadian Department of National Defence) has been undertaken by the IMP Group as the Turbo Tracker, and this, too, entered flight test during 1988. A mission avionics suite will be integrated in the Turbo Tracker demonstration aircraft to permit evaluation for the Canadian MRPA (Medium Range Patrol Aircraft) requirement. Markets for up to 60 fire-fighting and 150 ASW conversions are foreseen, 12 of the latter having been ordered by Brazil.

CONAIR TURBO FIRECAT

Dimensions: Span, 69 ft 8 in (21,23 m); length, 42 ft 3 in (12,88 m); height, 16 ft 3½ in (4,96 m); wing area, 485 sq ft (45,06 m²).

DASSAULT-BREGUET ATLANTIQUE 2 (ATL 2)

Country of Origin: France.

Type: Long-range maritime patrol aircraft.

Power Plant: Two 6,100 ehp Rolls-Royce Tyne Rty 20 Mk 21 turboprops.

Performance: Max speed, 402 mph (648 km/h) at optimum altitude, 368 mph (593 km/h) at sea level; max cruise, 345 mph (586 km/h) at 25,000 ft (7 620 m); normal patrol speed, 195 mph (315 km/h) at 5,000 ft (1 525 m); max initial climb (at 88,185 lb/ 40 000 kg), 2,000 ft/min (10,1 m/sec); service ceiling, 30,000 ft (9 145 m); typical ASW mission (at 97,665 lb with cruise to search area at 333 mph/537 km/h at 25,000 ft/7 620 m), 8-hr low-altitude patrol at 690 mls (1 110 km) from base, 5-hr low altitude patrol at 1,150 mls (1 850 km) from base; ferry range 5,635 mls (9 075 mls).

Weights: Empty equipped, 56,658 lb (25 700 kg); normal loaded weight, 97,442 lb (44 200 kg); max take-off, 101,850 lb (46 200 kg).

Accommodation: Normal flight crew of 12.

Armament: Up to eight Mk 46 homing torpedoes, nine 550-lb (250-kg) bombs or 12 depth charges and up to two AM 39 Exocet ASMs. Four underwing stations for up to 7,716 lb (3 500 kg) of stores.

Status: First of two prototypes (converted ATL 1s) flown 8 May 1981, and first series ATL 2 flown 19 October 1988. Sixteen ordered against requirement for 42, with first delivery scheduled for 1 June 1989 and production building up to one aircraft every two months.

Notes: The ATL2 is a modernised version of the ATL 1, production of which terminated in 1973 after completion of 87 series aircraft. Whereas the ATL1 was a multi-national programme, the ATL2 has so far been ordered solely by France's naval air arm.

DASSAULT-BREGUET ATLANTIQUE 2 (ATL 2)

Dimensions: Span, 122 ft 9¼ in (37,42 m); length, 103 ft 9 in (31,62 m); height, 35 ft 8¾ in (10,89 m); wing area, 1,295·3 sq ft (120,34 m²).

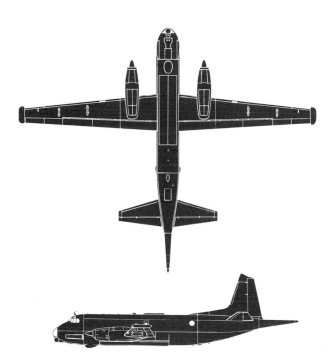

DASSAULT-BREGUET MIRAGE 2000N

Country of Origin: France.

Type: Tandem two-seat low-altitude strike aircraft.

Power Plant: One 14,460 lb st (6 500 kgp) dry and 21,385 lb st (9 700 kgp) reheat SNECMA M53-P2 turbofan.

Performance: Max speed (short endurance dash), 1,485 mph (2 390 km/h) above 36,090 ft (11 000 m), or Mach = 2·25, (continuous, 1,386 mph (2 230 km/h), or Mach 2·1, (low altitude without reheat and with ASMP), 695 mph (1 118 km/h), or Mach = 0·912; max initial climb, 59,055 ft/min (300 m/sec); time to 49,210 ft (15 000 m) and Mach = 2·0, 4·0 min; radius of action (with ASMP and two 374 Imp gal/1 700 l drop tanks), approx 930 mls (1 500 km).

Weights: Empty, 17,085 (7 750 kg); max take-off, 38,140 lb (17 300 kg).

Armament: One ASMP medium-range nuclear missile, or (non-ASMP version) up to 13,228 lb (6 000 kg) of conventional ordnance distributed between nine (five fuselage and four wing) stores stations, plus two self-defence Magic 2 AAMs.

Status: First of two prototypes flown on 2 February 1983, with production deliveries commencing on 10 February 1987, operational capability attained on 1 July 1988, and 31 delivered by beginning of 1989. Seventeen non-ASMP aircraft to be delivered during 1989, followed by 15 more plus six ASMP-equipped in 1990. Total procurement of 112 Mirage 2000Ns planned by French Air Force.

Notes: Optimised for the low-altitude penetration task with terrain-following and ground-mapping radar, the Mirage 2000N is being delivered in two versions, one equipped for the ASMP 300 kT nuclear missile and the other for conventional weapons.

DASSAULT-BREGUET MIRAGE 2000N

Dimensions: Span, 29 ft 11½ in (9,13 m); length, 47 ft 9 in (14,55 m); height, 16 ft 10¾ in (5,15 m); wing area, 441·3 sq ft (41,00 m²).

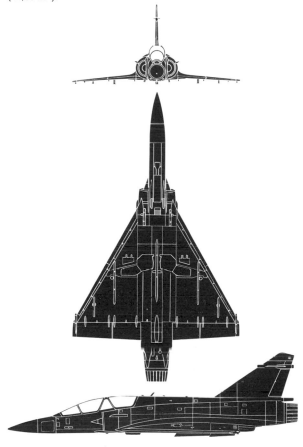

DASSAULT-BREGUET MYSTÈRE-FALCON 900

Country of Origin: France.
Type: Light corporate transport.
Power Plant: Three 4,500 lb st (2 040 kgp) Garrett TFE 731-5AR-1C turbofans.
Performance: Max speed (at 27,000 lb/12 250 kg), 574 mph (924 km/h) at 36,000 ft (10 975 m), or Mach = 0·87; max cruise, 554 mph (892 km/h) at 39,000 ft (11 890 m), or Mach = 0·84; econ cruise, 495 mph (797 km/h) at 37,000 ft (11 275 m), or Mach = 0·75; range (max payload and IFR reserves), 3,984 mls (6 412 km), (with 15 passengers), 4,329 mls (6 968 km), (with eight passengers), 4,491 mls (7 227 km).
Weights: Operational empty (typical), 23,248 lb (10 545 kg); max take-off, 45,500 lb (20 640 kg).
Accommodation: Flight crew of two and optional main cabin arrangements for 8–15 passengers, with maximum seating arrangement for 18 passengers in four rows three abreast.
Status: Two prototypes flown on 21 September 1984 and 30 August 1985, with first production aircraft following in March 1986, and first customer delivery on 19 December of that year.
Notes: The Mystère-Falcon 900 is the largest member of the Mystère-Falcon family of business executive transports and has been derived from the similarly-configured Falcon 50 (see 1982 edition). While sharing some limited component commonality, the 900 is scaled up approximately 10 per cent by comparison with the 50, and possesses more powerful engines. A long-range maritime surveillance version of the 900 is available and two examples of this variant have been ordered by Japan's Maritime Safety Agency for delivery during the course of 1989. The 900 has established class C1g records for climb and for maintaining altitude in level flight.

DASSAULT-BREGUET MYSTÈRE-FALCON 900

Dimensions: Span, 63 ft 5 in (19,33 m); length, 66 ft $3\frac{2}{3}$ in (20,21 m); height, 24 ft $9\frac{1}{4}$ in (7,55 m); wing area, 527·77 sq ft (49,03 m²).

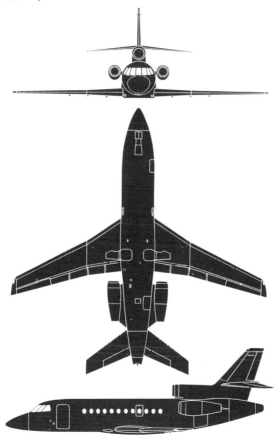

DASSAULT-BREGUET RAFALE A

Country of Origin: France.
Type: Single-seat advanced fighter technology demonstrator.
Power Plant: Two 16,000 lb st (7 258 kgp) reheat General Electric F404-GE-400 turbofans.
Performance: Max design speed, 1,320 mph (2 124 km/h) above 36,000 ft (10 975 m), or Mach = 2·0, 920 mph (1 480 km/h) at sea level, or Mach = 1·2.
Weights: Empty, 20,950 lb (9 500 kg); loaded (with two Magic and four Mica AAMs), 30,864 lb (14 000 kg); max take-off, 44,090 lb (20 000 kg).
Armament: Provision for one 30-mm cannon and 12 external stores stations. Typical air defence armament comprises four Mica medium-range AAMs (two mounted in tandem on the fuselage centreline and two mounted on rear lateral fuselage stations) and two Magic 2 short-range AAMs.
Status: Single Rafale A prototype flown on 4 July 1986. Five additional prototypes currently under development, including two single-seat and one two-seat Rafale D, and two single-seat Rafale M. Current planning calls for 250 Rafale Ds for the Air Force and 80 Rafale Ms for the Navy, with deliveries commencing 1996 and 1998 respectively.
Notes: Built to demonstrate technologies applicable to the next generation of tactical combat aircraft, the Rafale (Squall) A is providing the basis for a multi-role fighter (Rafale D) for the French Air Force to replace the Mirage IIIE and Jaguar, and a shipboard fighter (Rafale M) for the French Navy to succeed the Crusader and Etendard IVP. The first of five additional prototypes powered by the SNECMA M88 Mk 2 is to enter flight test in 1991, and series production is due to begin in 1994. The series Rafales will be marginally smaller than the Rafale A and will have an operational empty weight of some 18,960 lb (8 600 kg).

DASSAULT-BREGUET RAFALE A

Dimensions: Span (including wingtip missiles), 36 ft $8\frac{1}{8}$ in (11,18 m); length, 51 ft 10 in (15,79 m); height, 16 ft $11\frac{7}{8}$ in (5,18 m); wing area, 506 sq ft (47,00 m²).

DASSAULT-BREGUET/DORNIER ALPHA JET 2

Countries of Origin: France and Federal Germany.
Type: Tandem two-seat advanced trainer and light tactical support aircraft.
Power Plant: Two 3,175 lb st (1 440 kgp) SNECMA/Turbo-méca Larzac 04-C20 turbofans.
Performance: Max speed, 572 mph (920 km/h) at 32,800 ft (10 000 m), or Mach = 0·86, 645 mph (1 038 km/h) at sea level, or Mach = 0·896; max initial climb, 11,220 ft/min (57 m/sec); service ceiling, 48,000 ft (14 630 m); tactical radius (LO-LO-LO with centreline gun pod and underwing ordnance), 242 mls (390 km), (plus two 137·5 Imp gal/625 l drop tanks), 391 mls (630 km), (HI-LO-HI), 668 mls (1 075 km).
Weights: Empty equipped, 7,749 lb (3 515 km); max take-off, 17,637 lb (8 000 kg).
Armament: More than 75 basic weapon configurations for armament training and tactical support, with (when flown as single-seater) max of 5,510 lb (2 500 kg) of ordnance distributed between five stations.
Status: Alpha Jet 2 entered flight test on 9 April 1982. Four delivered to Egypt in following year by parent companies, and co-production with Egyptian industry which assembled 37 from CKD kits in training (MS1) and attack (MS2) versions. Six of the latter version delivered to Cameroun.
Notes: The Alpha Jet 2 is an upgraded dual-role derivative of the original Alpha Jet of which 512 were built with deliveries completed in June 1988. The Lancier is an extended-capability version of the Alpha Jet 2 for day/night attack and anti-shipping strike, and the Alpha Jet 3 is an advanced training system version with state-of-the-art cockpit.

DASSAULT-BREGUET/DORNIER ALPHA JET 2

Dimensions: Span, 29 ft 11 in (9,11 m); length, 40 ft 3 in (12,29 m); height, 13 ft 9 in (4,19 m); wing area, 188 sq ft (17,50 m²).

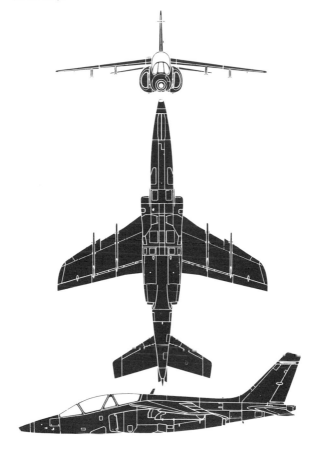

DORNIER DO 228-200

Country of Origin: Federal Germany.
Type: Light regional and utility transport, medevac and maritime patrol aircraft.
Power Plant: Two 715 shp Garrett TPE 331-5-252D turbo-props.
Performance: (228-202) Max cruise speed, 266 mph (428 km/h) at 10,000 ft (3 050 m), 230 mph (370 km/h) at sea level; range cruise, 207 mph (333 km/h) at 10,000 ft (3 050 m); max initial climb, 1,800 ft/min (9,1 m/sec); range (with 19 passengers and reserves), 691 mls (1 112 km).
Weights: Operational empty (including two pilots), 8,153 lb (3 698 kg); max take-off, 13,669 lb (6 200 kg).
Accommodation: Flight crew of two and standard arrangement (228–202) for 19 passengers (14 individual seats with central aisle, two paired seats and three seats along rear bulkhead).
Status: Prototype 228-100 flown 28 March 1981, with prototype 228-200 following on 9 May 1981. Customer deliveries commencing February 1982, with some 160 delivered by beginning of 1989. Licence manufacture being undertaken by Kanpur Division of Hindustan Aircraft, first Indian-assembled aircraft (228-201) flown on 31 January 1986. Thirty-three being built at Kanpur for the Indian Coast Guard, more than 50 for the Indian Air Force and some 24 for the Indian Navy, production rate being two monthly.
Notes: The 228-100 is the basic version of this multi-role aircraft, the -200 having a lengthened fuselage. The 228-101 has a reinforced fuselage for higher operating weights, this modification also being featured by the -201. The -202 described above offers increases in payload/range performance by comparison with the 228-201 (illustrated above and on opposite page), and the 228-203F is a dedicated freighter version. A specialised maritime patrol version is being supplied to the Indian Navy, and paratroop transport, signals intelligence and medevac versions are available.

DORNIER DO 228-200

Dimensions: Span, 55 ft 7 in (16,97 m); length, 54 ft 4 in (16,56 m); height, 15 ft 9 in (4,86 m); wing area, 344·46 sq ft (32,00 m²).

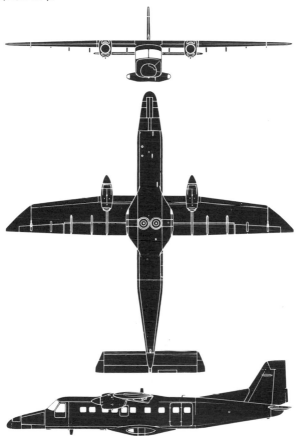

EMBRAER EMB-120 BRASILIA

Country of Origin: Brazil.

Type: Short-haul regional transport.

Power Plant: Two 1,800 shp Pratt & Whitney Canada PW118 turboprops.

Performance: Max speed, 378 mph (608 km/h) at 20,000 ft (6 100 m); max cruise, 343 mph (552 km/h) at 20,000 ft (6 100 m); long-range cruise, 299 mph (482 km/h) at 25,000 ft (7 620 m); max initial climb, 2,120 ft/min (10,77 m/sec); service ceiling, 29,800 ft (1 750 km), (max fuel and 21 passengers), 1,853 mls (2 982 km).

Weights: Empty equipped, 15,586 lb (7 070 kg); max take-off, 25,353 lb (11 500 kg).

Accommodation: Flight crew of two and standard arrangement for 30 passengers in three-abreast seating. Optional arrangements include all-cargo interior, or mixed-traffic versions with seating for 24 to 26 passengers.

Status: First of three prototypes was flown on 27 July 1983, with first customer delivery (to Atlantic Southeast Airlines) following August 1985. Production tempo five aircraft monthly at the beginning of 1989, with 115 aircraft delivered against orders for 199 and options on 158 aircraft. One hundredth delivered October 1988.

Notes: The Brazilian Air Force has ordered eight EMB-120s as C-97 personnel and freight transports and has a requirement for a further 16. It has also taken delivery of two as VC-97 VIP transports. A 'hot-and-high' version with more powerful PW118A engines and reduced structural weight became available in 1988, first customer being SkyWest.

EMBRAER EMB-120 BRASILIA

Dimensions: Span, 64 ft 10¾ in (19,78 m); length, 65 ft 7½ in (20,00 m); height, 20 ft 10 in (6,35 m); wing area, 424·42 sq ft (39,43 m²).

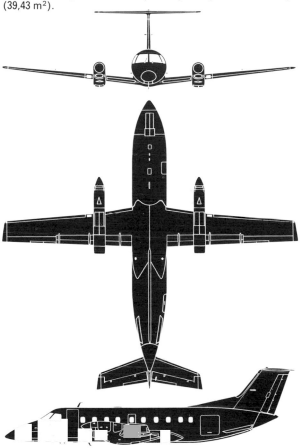

EMBRAER EMB-312 TUCANO

Country of Origin: Brazil.
Type: Tandem two-seat basic trainer.
Power Plant: One 750 shp Pratt & Whitney Canada PT6A-25C turboprop.
Performance: (At 5,622 lb/2 550 kg) Max speed, 278 mph (448 km/h) at 10,000 ft (3 050 m); max cruise, 255 mph (411 km/h); econ cruise, 198 mph (319 km/h); max initial climb, 2,331 ft/min (11,84 m/sec); service ceiling, 30,000 ft (9 150 m); max range (max internal fuel and 30 min reserves), 1,145 mls (1 844 km) at 20,000 ft (6 100 m); ferry range (with two 145 Imp gal/660 l underwing tanks), 2,069 mls (3 330 km).
Weights: Basic empty, 3,991 lb (1 810 kg); max take-off, 5,622 lb (2 550 kg), (with external stores), 7,000 lb (3 175 kg).
Armament: (Light strike and weapons training) Up to 2,205 lb (1 000 kg) of ordnance between four wing stations.
Status: First of four prototypes flown on 15 August 1980, with deliveries (to Brazilian Air Force) commencing September 1983. More than 400 delivered by beginning of 1989 when production was 4·5 monthly (this including 100 supplied as kits for assembly in Egypt) and orders and options totalled 593 aircraft as follows: Brazil 118 (+50 options), Egypt 40 (+40), Honduras 12, Iraq 80 (+20), Argentina (30), Peru (20), Paraguay (6), Venezuela (32) and UK 130 (+15).
Notes: Licence manufacture of a re-engined and upgraded version for the RAF being undertaken in UK (see pages 194–5). Follow-on orders with two existing operators (including 15 for Argentina) were being negotiated at beginning of 1989, and procurement of 75 is planned by the French Air Force, with deliveries commencing in 1990.

EMBRAER EMB-312 TUCANO

Dimensions: Span, 36 ft 6½ in (11,14 m); length, 32 ft 4¼ in (9,86 m); height, 11 ft 7⅞ in (3,40 m); wing area, 208·82 sq ft (19,40 m²).

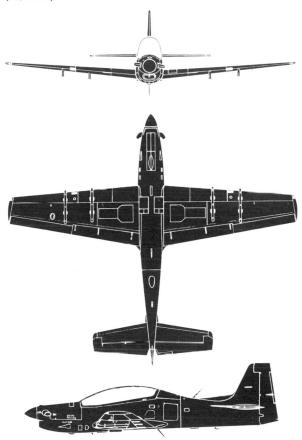

EMBRAER-FAMA CBA-123

Countries of Origin: Brazil and Argentina.
Type: Light regional airliner and corporate transport.
Power Plant: Two 1,300 shp Garrett TPF351-20 turboprops.
Performance: (Manufacturer's estimates) Max cruise speed, 404 mph (650 km/h) at 30,000 ft (9 145 m); initial climb, 2,700 ft/min (13,72 m/sec); service ceiling, 40,000 ft (12 190 m); range (with 19 passengers and IFR reserves), 868 mls (1 396 km).
Weights: Operational empty, 12,434 lb (5 640 kg); max take-off, 18,739 lb (8 500 kg).
Accommodation: Flight crew of two and standard arrangement for 19 passengers three abreast with four seats on rear cabin bulkhead.
Status: The first of three prototypes scheduled to fly (in Brazil) in December 1989, with second flying (also in Brazil) in January 1990, and third (in Argentina) in July 1990. To be produced on assembly lines in both Brazil and Argentina, with certification and initial customer deliveries in 1991.
Notes: The CBA-123 is being developed jointly by Embraer of Brazil and FAMA of Argentina, each company establishing final assembly lines without component manufacturing duplication. The CBA-123 is innovative in having its turboprops pylon-mounted on the rear fuselage and driving six-bladed, scimitar-shaped pusher propellers. Embraer is responsible for two-thirds and FAMA for one-third under the work-sharing agreement, and marketing is to be split between the two companies, FAMA having rights in Latin America and some African countries.

EMBRAER-FAMA CBA-123

Dimensions: Span, 58 ft 1⅔ in (17,72 m); length, 58 ft 3⅗ in (17,77 m); height, 20 ft 8¾ in (6,32 m); wing area, 292·79 sq ft (27,20 m²).

ENAER T-35 PILLÁN

Country of Origin: Chile.
Type: Tandem two-seat primary/basic trainer.
Power Plant: One 300 hp Textron Lycoming AEIO-540-K1K5 six-cylinder horizontally-opposed engine.
Performance: (T-35A) Max speed, 193 mph (311 km/h) at sea level; cruise (75% power), 166 mph (266 km/h) at 8,800 ft (2 680 m), (55% power), 159 mph (255 km/h) at 16,800 ft (5 120 m); max initial climb, 1,525 ft/min (7,75 m/sec); service ceiling, 19,160 ft (5 840 m); range (75% power with 45 min reserves), 679 mls (1 093 km), (55% power and 45 min reserves), 748 mls (1 204 km).
Weights: Empty equipped, 2,050 lb (9 30 kg); max take-off, 2,950 lb (1 338 kg).
Status: First of two (Piper-developed) prototypes flown on 6 March 1981, and first of three ENAER-assembled pre-series aircraft flown 30 January 1982, with first series aircraft following 28 December 1984. Completion of 80 (60 T-35As and 20 T-35Bs) for Chilean Air Force scheduled for early 1989. Forty supplied as kits to CASA (as T-35C) for assembly for Spanish Air Force, and four (T-35D) delivered to Panamanian Air Force.
Notes: The Pillán (Devil), designed under contract by Piper, embodies standard components of PA-28, PA-31 and PA-32. The T-35B has avionics for IFR instruction and T-35C serves with the Spanish Air Force as the E.26 Tamiz (Grader).

ENAER T-35 PILLÁN

Dimensions: Span, 29 ft 0 in (8,84 m); length, 26 ft 3 in (8,00 m); height, 8 ft 8 in (2,64 m); wing area, 147·34 sq ft (13,69 m²).

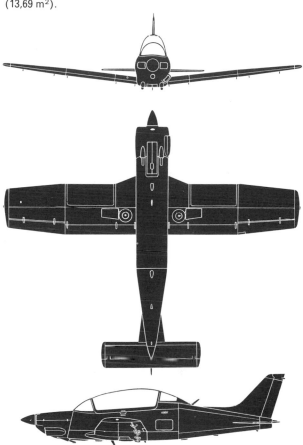

FAMA IA 63 PAMPA

Country of Origin: Argentina.
Type: Tandem two-seat basic/advanced trainer.
Power Plant: One 3,500 lb st (1 588 kgp) Garrett TFE-371-2-2N turbofan.
Performance: Max speed, 509 mph (819 km/h) at 22,965 ft (7 000 m), 469 mph (755 km/h) at sea level; max cruise, 464 mph (747 km/h) at 13,125 ft (4 000 m); max initial climb, 5,950 ft/min (30,23 m/sec); service ceiling, 43,325 ft (12 900 m); range, 932 mls (1 500 km) at 345 mph (556 km/h) at 13,125 ft (4 000 m).
Weights: Empty, 6,219 lb (2 821 kg); max take-off, 11,023 lb (5 000 kg).
Armament: (Armament training or light attack) One 30-mm cannon pod on fuselage centreline. Maximum ordnance load (including cannon) of 2,557 lb (1 160 kg) distributed between centreline and four wing stations.
Status: First of three prototypes flown on 6 October 1984, and first three series aircraft delivered on 15 March 1988, with total of nine scheduled to have been completed by the beginning of 1989 against initial contract for 18 aircraft and Argentine Air Force requirement for 68.
Notes: The Pampa was developed on behalf of the Argentine government by Dornier of Federal Germany, this company continuing to provide assistance to the FAMA (Fábrica Argentina de Materiales Aeroespaciales) in the manufacture and progressive development of this aircraft. The third prototype Pampa differs from the preceding prototypes in having the Martin-Baker ejection seats replaced by Stencel seats (now standardised) and provision for armament. A version for the light attack role with an uprated engine – probably the 4,300 lb st (1 950 kgp) TFE731-5 – is projected and consideration has allegedly been given to a shipboard version. Various instructional and light attack versions are being offered for export.

FAMA IA 63 PAMPA

Dimensions: Span, 31 ft $9\frac{1}{2}$ in (9,69 m); length, 35 ft $9\frac{1}{4}$ in (10,90 m); height, 14 ft $0\frac{3}{4}$ in (4,29 m); wing area, 168·24 sq ft (15,63 m²).

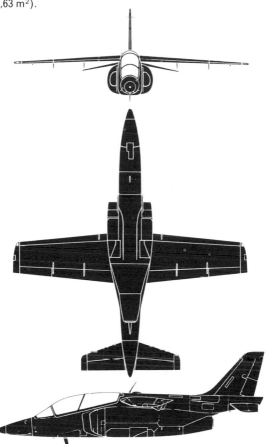

FFV/MFI BA-14 STARLING

Country of Origin: Sweden.
Type: Side-by-side two-seat light instructional, touring and multi-role aircraft.
Power Plant: One 115 hp Textron Lycoming O-235-L or 160 hp O-320-D four-cylinder horizontally-opposed engine.
Performance: Max speed (115 hp), 144 mph (232 km/h) at sea level, (160 hp) 173 mph (278 km/h) at sea level; max initial climb, (115 hp) 600 ft/min (3,05 m/sec), (160 hp) 900 ft/min (4,57 m/sec).
Weights: Empty (115 hp), 1,058 lb (480 kg), (160 hp), 1,113 lb (505 kg); max take-off (115 hp normal category), 1,800 lb (815 kg), (160 hp), 2,095 lb (950 kg).
Status: The first prototype BA-14 flew for the first time on 25 August 1988. No production plans had been announced by the beginning of 1989.
Notes: Designed by Bjorn Andreasson and built as a collaborative programme between Malmö Research and Development and FFV Aerotech, the Starling is of all-composite construction, using glass-reinforced plastic for the fuselage and wings, with the caps of the wing spars reinforced by carbonfibre. The aim is to achieve low structural weight, reduced corrosion, and ease of maintenance and repair. Although primarily seen as a touring and training aircraft, the Starling also possesses light agricultural and reconnaissance capabilities. The fuselage incorporates a downward-hinged rear door permitting the loading of light items of freight or a casualty stretcher. For the agricultural mission a hopper may be fitted in the fuselage and spray bars mounted beneath the wing. Wing hardpoints allow for supply packs and other stores to be carried for air-dropping, or for the application of reconnaissance pods and other sensors. The Starling is intended, in part, to provide FFV with experience of composites for primary structure design and production.

FFV/MFI BA-14 STARLING

Dimensions: Span, 37 ft 4 in (11,38 m); length, 21 ft 6 in (6,56 m); height, 8 ft 10 in (2,70 m).

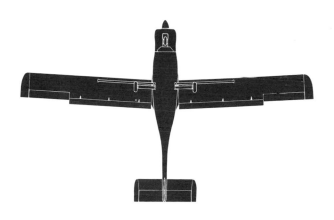

FOKKER 50

Country of Origin: Netherlands.

Type: Regional commercial transport.

Power Plant: Two 2,250 shp Pratt & Whitney (Canada) PW125B turboprops.

Performance: Max cruise speed, 330 mph (532 km/h) at 16,000 ft (4 875 m); long-range cruise, 282 mph (454 km/h); max operational altitude, 25,000 ft (7 620 m); range (with 50 passengers and reserves), 723 mls (1 163 km) at 41,865 lb (18 990 kg) at long-range cruise, 1,828 mls (2 943 km) at 45,900 lb (20 820 kg) at long-range cruise.

Weights: Operational empty, 28,090 lb (12 742 kg); max take-off (standard), 41,865 lb (18 990 kg), (optional), 45,900 lb (20 820 kg).

Accommodation: Flight crew of two and standard arrangement for 50 passengers four abreast, with optional high-density seating for 58 passengers.

Status: First of two prototypes (based on F27 airframes) flown on 28 December 1985, with first production aircraft following on 13 February 1987, and first customer delivery (to DLT) on 7 August 1987. Total of 93 (plus 31 options) ordered by beginning of 1989 when production rate was 30 annually, with 38 delivered.

Notes: The Fokker 50 is based on the F27-500 Friendship (see 1982 edition), but embodies significant design and structural changes, making extensive use of composites and utilising new-technology engines driving six-bladed propellers. Under consideration at the beginning of 1989 was the Fokker 50-200 with an 8·86-ft (2,70-m) fuselage stretch and 62-seat capacity.

FOKKER 50

Dimensions: Span, 95 ft $1\frac{3}{4}$ in (29,00 m); length, 82 ft 10 in (25,25 m); height, 27 ft $3\frac{1}{2}$ in (8,32 m); wing area, 753·5 sq ft (70,00 m²).

FOKKER 100

Country of Origin: Netherlands.
Type: Short/medium-haul commercial transport.
Power Plant: Two 13,850 lb st (6 282 kgp) Rolls-Royce RB183 Tay 620-15 or 15,100 lb st (6 850 kgp) Tay 650-15 turbofans.
Performance: Max cruise speed, 535 mph (861 km/h) at 24,200 ft (7 375 m); range cruise, 465 mph (748 km/h) at 35,000 ft (10 670 m); range (at 95,000 lb/43 090 kg with 107 passengers), 1,543 mls (2 483 km), (at 98,000 lb/44 450 kg with 107 passengers), 1,842 mls (2 965 km).
Weights: (Tay 620) Typical operational empty, 53,700 lb (24 360 kg); max take-off, 95,000 lb (43 090 kg); (Tay 650) typical operational empty, 54,100 lb (24 540 kg); max take-off, 98,000 lb (44 450 kg).
Accommodation: Flight crew of two and standard arrangement for 107 passengers seated five abreast with offset aisle.
Status: First of two prototypes flown 30 November 1986, with second following on 25 February 1987. First customer delivery (to Swissair) on 29 February 1988, with total of 11 delivered during course of year, 33 to be delivered during 1989, and 39 during 1990. Orders totalled 118 aircraft (plus 88 on option) by beginning of 1989.
Notes: The Fokker 100 is technically a derivative of the F28 (see 1985 edition), but makes extensive use of advanced technology, has new systems and equipment, new engines, a lengthened fuselage and aerodynamically redesigned wings.

FOKKER 100

Dimensions: Span, 92 ft 1½ in (28,08 m); length, 116 ft 6¾ in (35,53 m); height, 27 ft 10½ in (8,60 m); wing area, 1,006·4 sq ft (93,50 m²).

FUJI KM-2D

Country of Origin: Japan.
Type: Side-by-side two-seat primary trainer.
Power Plant: One 350 shp Allison 250-B17D turboprop.
Performance: Max speed, 216 mph (348 km/h) at sea level, 222 mph (358 km/h) at 8,000 ft (2440 m); initial climb, 1,700 ft/min (8,63 m/sec); range, 587 mls (945 km).
Weights: Empty, 2,386 lb (1 082 kg); loaded (aerobatic), 3,495 lb (1 585 kg), (utility), 3,980 lb (1 805 kg).
Status: The prototype KM-2D, a re-engined company-owned KM-2, was first flown on 28 June 1984, and the first series KM-2D embodying extensive cabin redesign was flown on 27 April 1988. A contract for conversion of the entire Japanese Maritime Self-Defence Force fleet of 32 piston-engined KM-2 trainers to KM-2D standard was awarded in March 1987, with deliveries scheduled to commence early 1989.
Notes: The KM-2D is the result of incremental development and redesign of the Beechcraft B45 Mentor, licence manufacture of 126 examples of which was undertaken by Fuji after assembly of 50 from component kits. A four-seat Fuji derivative of the Mentor was produced for the liaison role as the LM-1, and the fundamentally similar KM-2 (340 hp Lycoming IGSO-480-A1C6 piston engine) was procured by the Maritime Self-Defence Force as the service's standard primary trainer. Re-engined with an Allison 250-B17D turboprop and fitted with enlarged and swept vertical tail surfaces, one example became the prototype KM-2D and this obtained JCAB certification (Aerobatic and Utility categories) in February 1985.

FUJI KM-2D

Dimensions: Span, 32 ft 11¼ in (10,04 m); length, 27 ft 8¼ in (8,44 m); height, 9 ft 8½ in (2,96 m); wing area, 177·6 sq ft (16,50 m²).

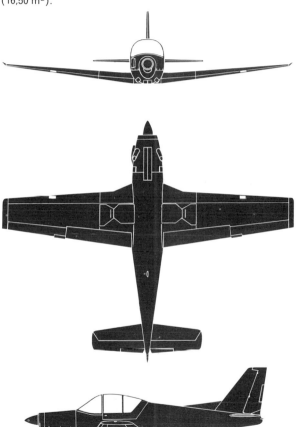

GENERAL DYNAMICS F-16 FIGHTING FALCON

Country of Origin: USA.

Type: (F-16C) Single-seat multi-role fighter and (F-16D) two-seat operational trainer.

Power Plant: One 14,370 lb st (6 518 kgp) dry and 23,450 lb st (10 637 kgp) reheat Pratt & Whitney F100-PW-220 or 14,000 lb st (6 350 kgp) dry and 27,600 lb st (12 520 kgp) reheat General Electric F110-GE-100 turbofan.

Performance: (F-100-powered F-16C) Max speed (short endurance dash), 1,333 mph (2 145 km/h) at 40,000 ft (12 190 m), or Mach = 2·02, (sustained), 1,247 mph (2 007 km/h), or Mach = 1·89; tactical radius (HI-LO-HI interdiction on internal fuel with six 500-lb/227-kg bombs), 360 mls (580 km); ferry range (max external fuel), 2,450 mls (3 943 km).

Weights: Empty, 18,335 lb (8 316 kg); max take-off (air-air), 25,071 lb (11 372 kg), (with max external load), 42,300 lb (19 187 kg).

Armament: One 20-mm rotary cannon and (intercept) two to six AIM-9 Sidewinder AAMs, or (interdiction) up to 12,430 lb (5 638 kg) ordnance between nine stations.

Status: First of two (YF-16) prototypes flown 20 January 1974, and first production aircraft (F-16A) flown 7 August 1978, with first F-16C being delivered 19 July 1984. Total of 3,023 F-16s (all versions) ordered by beginning of 1989 of which more than 2,000 delivered. Customers as follows: Bahrain (12), Belgium (160), Denmark (70), Egypt (120), Greece (40), Indonesia (12), Israel (150), Netherlands (214), Norway (74), Pakistan (40), Singapore (8), South Korea (36), Thailand (18), Turkey (160), Venezuela (24) and USA (1 885).

Notes: F-16C/D are current basic production versions with common engine bay for either F100 or F110.

GENERAL DYNAMICS F-16 FIGHTING FALCON

Dimensions: Span (over missile launchers), 31 ft 0 in (9,45 m); length, 49 ft 4 in (15,03 m); height, 16 ft 8⅖ in (5,09 m); wing area, 300 sq ft (27,87 m²).

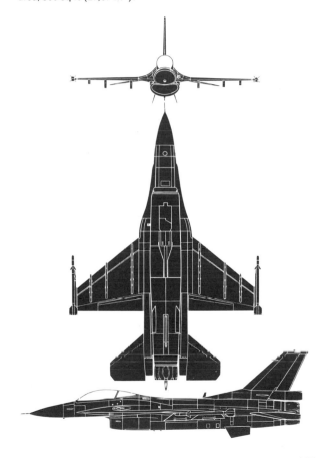

GRUMMAN E-2C HAWKEYE

Country of Origin: USA.
Type: Shipboard or shore-based airborne early warning, surface surveillance and strike control aircraft.
Power Plant: Two 4,910 ehp Allison T56-A-425 or 5,250 ehp T56-A-427 turboprops.
Performance: (-425 engines at max take-off) Max speed, 372 mph (598 km/h); max cruise, 358 mph (576 km/h); max initial climb, 2,515 ft/min (12,8 m/sec); service ceiling, 30,800 ft (9 390 m); time of station (200 mls/320 km from base), 3–4 hrs; ferry range, 1,604 mls (2 580 km).
Weights: Empty, 38,063 lb (17 265 kg); max take-off, 51,933 lb (23 556 kg).
Accommodation: Normal flight crew of two and (main compartment) combat information centre officer, air control officer and radar operator.
Status: First of two E-2C prototypes flown 20 January 1971, with first production aircraft following on 23 September 1972. Total of 144 ordered by US Navy of which 107 delivered by beginning of 1989. Four supplied to Israel, eight to Japan (with five more to be delivered), five to Egypt and four to Singapore. Production continuing at rate of six annually.
Notes: The E-2C has been evolved from the E-2A (56 built with 52 upgraded to E-2B standard) and differs fundamentally in supplanting the 'blue water' capable APS-96 radar system with APS-120 capable of target detection and tracking over land. The improved AP-138 was retrofitted from 1983, and this gave place to AP-139 in new production E-2Cs from 1988. The extended detection range APS-145, which is less susceptible to overland clutter, is scheduled to be retrofitted to all aircraft from 1990. From 1987, the uprated T56-A-427 turboprop has been standardised, and, during 1988, the central computer has been upgraded, and improved IFF and enhanced displays have been introduced.

GRUMMAN E-2C HAWKEYE

Dimensions: Span, 80 ft 7 in (24,56 m); length, 57 ft 7 in (17,55 m); height, 18 ft 4 in (5,69 m); wing area, 700 sq ft (65,03 m²).

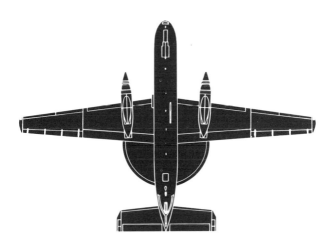

GRUMMAN F-14A (PLUS) TOMCAT

Country of Origin: USA.
Type: Two-seat shipboard multi-role fighter.
Power Plant: Two 14,000 lb st (6 350 kgp) dry and 23,100 lb st (10 478 kgp) General Electric F110-GE-400 turbofans.
Performance: Max speed (with four semi-recessed AIM-7 AAMs) 1,544 mph (2 485 km/h) at 40,000 ft (12 190 m), or Mach = 2·34, 912 mph (1 468 km/h) at sea level, or Mach = 1·2; intercept radius (at Mach = 1·3), 510 mls (820 km); combat air patrol loiter time (with external fuel), 2·7 hrs.
Weights: (Estimated) Empty, 42,000 lb (19 050 kg); max take-off, 75,000 lb (34 020 kg).
Armament: One 20-mm rotary cannon and (typical) four AIM-54C Phoenix (beneath fuselage) or four AIM-7 Sparrow (partially submerged in fuselage underside), plus four AIM-9 Sidewinder or two additional Phoenix or Sparrow missiles on fixed-glove pylons.
Status: First of two F-14A (Plus) prototypes flown on 29 September 1986, with first deliveries to US Navy in April 1988. Production of 38 F-14A (Plus) Tomcats, first of which flown on 14 November 1987, is following manufacture of 557 F-14As (including 12 R&D aircraft), production of this version having terminated in April 1987. With completion of F-14A (Plus) deliveries in May 1990, production will have switched to the definitive F-14D.
Notes: The F-14A (Plus) is an interim upgrade of the F-14A pending introduction of the F-14D, current planning calling for procurement of 12 of the latter annually plus conversion of six F-14As to F-14D standards each year. Whereas the F-14A (Plus) is essentially the F-14A re-engined, the F-14D will have the new engines plus upgraded avionics. A total of 127 new-production F-14Ds is planned, plus remanufacture of some 400 earlier aircraft to similar standards.

118

GRUMMAN F-14A (PLUS) TOMCAT

Dimensions: Span (20 deg sweep), 64 ft 1½ in (19,55 m), (68 deg sweep), 38 ft 2½ in (11,65 m); length, 62 ft 8 in (19,10 m); height, 16 ft 0 in (4,88 m); wing area, 565 sq ft (52,49 m²).

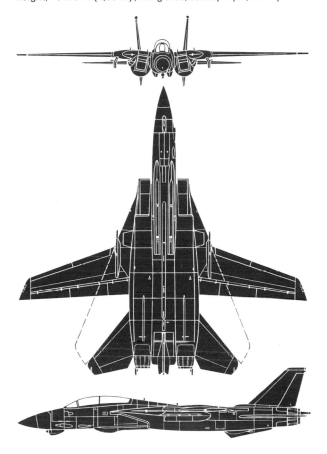

GULFSTREAM AEROSPACE GULFSTREAM
SRA-4

Country of Origin: USA.

Type: Multi-role special missions aircraft.

Power Plant: Two 13,850 lb st (6 282 kgp) Rolls-Royce Tay 611-8 turbofans.

Performance: Max cruise speed, 586 mph (943 km/h) at 31,000 ft (9 450 m); long-range cruise, 528 mph (850 km/h); max initial climb, 4,000 ft/min (20,32 m/sec); service ceiling, 51,000 ft (15 545 m); range (three crew, IFR reserves and 9,200 lb/4 173 kg freight), 5,180 mls (8 336 km), (with 10 passengers), 3,745 mls (6 027 km), (with 19 passengers), 4,320 mls (6 952 km).

Weights: Bare empty, 35,500 lb (16 103 kg); typical operational empty, 42,500 lb (19 277 kg); max take-off, 73,200 lb (33 203 kg).

Accommodation: Three crew and (priority cargo) up to 9,200 lb (4 173 kg) of freight or (administrative transport) 10–19 passengers, or (Medevac) two flying crew, three attendants and 15 casualty stretchers, or (maritime patrol) two flying crew and six mission crew, or (electronic warfare) four mission crew.

Status: Partially-developed prototype (based on Gulfstream IV corporate transport) under test mid-1988.

Notes: The SRA-4 is a derivative of the Gulfstream IV (see 1988 edition) corporate transport which is currently being built at a rate of five monthly, with some 85 delivered by the beginning of 1989. The special missions that the SRA-4 is intended to perform include electronic warfare support (the accompanying illustrations depicting it in this form), surveillance (in which form it can fly 9·24 hours on station at 33,000–47,000 ft/10 060–14 325 m) and maritime patrol (six hours on station at 528 mls/850 km from base). Late 1988, the SRA-4 had been tendered to meet a US Navy electronic warfare support aircraft requirement.

GULFSTREAM AEROSPACE GULFSTREAM SRA-4

Dimensions: Span, 77 ft 10 in (23,72 m); length, 88 ft 4 in (26,90 m); height, 24 ft 10 in (7,60 m); wing area, 950·39 sq ft (88,29 m²).

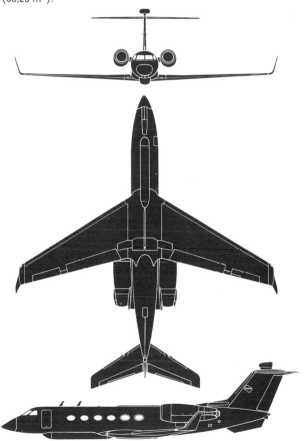

GULFSTREAM/SWEARINGEN SA-30 FANJET

Country of Origin: USA.

Type: Light corporate transport.

Power Plant: Two 1,800 lb st (816 kgp) Williams International FJ44 turbofans.

Performance: (Manufacturer's estimates) Max cruise speed, 518 mph plus (834 km/h plus); long-range cruise, 475 mph (764 km/h); certified ceiling, 41,000 ft (12 495 m); range (IFR), 2,105 mls (3 387 km), (VFR) 2,496 mls (4 017 km).

Weights: Empty equipped, 5,198 lb (2 358 kg); max take-off, 9,250 lb (4 196 kg).

Accommodation: Pilot and co-pilot/passenger on flight deck and typical main cabin arrangement for four passengers in individual seats. Optional six-passenger cabin arrangement.

Status: First prototype scheduled to enter flight test during third quarter of 1989, with FAA certification and initial customer deliveries in 1991.

Notes: The SA-30, which is being developed by Swearingen Engineering and Technology, Inc, and will be produced and marketed by Gulfstream Aerospace, is an advanced-technology, low-cost business executive aircraft. It is believed that an initial market exists for at least one thousand aircraft in this category if the anticipated combination of price and performance can be held. The wing will incorporate high-lift surfaces enabling the SA-30 to land at speeds normally associated with turboprop-powered corporate aircraft.

GULFSTREAM/SWEARINGEN SA-30 FANJET

Dimensions: Span, 36 ft 4 in (11,07 m); length, 41 ft $10\frac{7}{8}$ in (12,77 m); height, 12 ft 11 in (3,94 m); wing area, 164.9 sq.ft (15,32 m²).

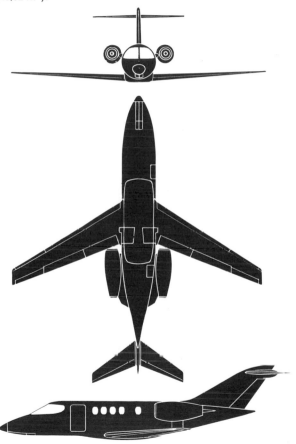

ILYUSHIN IL-76 (CANDID)

Country of Origin: USSR.

Type: Heavy-duty medium/long-haul military and commercial freighter and troop transport.

Power Plant: Four 26,455 lb st (12 000 kgp) Soloviev D-30KP-1 turbofans.

Performance: (Il-76TD) Max speed, 528 mph (850 km/h) at 32,810 ft (10 000 m); max cruise, 497 mph (800 km/h) at 29,500–42,650 ft (9 000–13 000 m); range (with max fuel), 4,908 mls (7 898 km); nominal range (with 105,820-lb/48 000-kg payload and 45 min reserves), 1,740 mls (2 800 km).

Weights: (Il-76TD) Max take-off, 418,875 lb (190 000 kg).

Accommodation: Normal flight crew of seven (including two freight handlers). Modules used for quick configuration changes, each able to accommodate 30 passengers in four-abreast seating, casualty stretchers or cargo. Three such modules may be carried.

Status: First of four prototypes flown in 25 March 1971, with production deliveries to both Aeroflot and the SovAF following 1974. Some 125 in service with Aeroflot and about 370 with the SovAF by beginning of 1989, when production was continuing at 4·0–4·5 monthly. Military versions delivered to Czechoslovakia, India, Iraq and Poland.

Notes: Progressive developments of the Il-76 have included the Il-76T with additional fuel tankage and Il-76TD with further increases in fuel, payload and max take-off weight (all Candid-A), and the military Il-76M and MD (both Candid-B) with rear turret containing two 23-mm cannon. The Il-78 Midas is a three-point flight refuelling tanker version which entered SovAF service in 1987. This has refuelling pods beneath the outer wings and a hose-reel in the rear fuselage.

Dimensions: Span, 165 ft 8⅓ in (50,50 m); length, 152 ft 10 ¼ in (46,59 m); height, 48 ft 5⅕ in (14,76 m); wing area, 3,229·2 sq ft (300,00 m²).

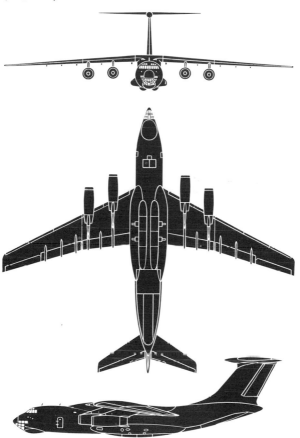

ILYUSHIN IL-96-300

Country of Origin: USSR.

Type: Long-haul commercial airliner.

Power Plant: Four 29,762 lb st (13 500 kgp) Soloviev PS-90A turbofans.

Performance: (Manufacturer's estimates) Max cruise speed, 559 mph (900 km/h) at 39,700 ft (12 100 m); econ cruise, 528 mph (850 km/h) at 33,135 ft (10 100 m); range (with reserves and max payload), 4,660 mls (7 500 km), (with reserves and 66,140-lb/30 000-kg payload), 5,592 mls (9 000 km), (with reserves and 33,070-lb/15 000-kg payload), 6,835 mls (11 000 km).

Weights: Basic operational, 257,936 lb (117 000 kg); max take-off, 476,200 lb (216 000 kg).

Accommodation: Flight crew of three with all-tourist class arrangement for 300 passengers in three rows three abreast, typical mixed-class arrangement comprising 22 first class, 40 business class and 173 tourist class passengers.

Status: First of five prototypes flown on 28 September 1988, with initial customer (Aeroflot) deliveries in 1991, and current planning for 60–70 to be built by 1995. Both CSA and LOT have indicated their intention to procure the Il-96.

Notes: Possessing a close family resemblance to the Il-86 (see 1988 edition), but fundamentally a new design with a supercritical wing and triple-redundant digital fly-by-wire controls, the Il-96-300 is the first of a family of airliners. To have the fully-rated (35,280 lb st/16 000 kgp) PS-90A turbofans, the Il-96-350 and -400 will be stretched versions which will retain the same wing, max take-off weight rising in stages to 573,192 lb (260 000 kg). The Il-96 is built at Voronezh, the wing slats, pylons for the engine pods, the tail fin and tailplane being manufactured in Poland by PZL Mielec.

ILYUSHIN IL-96-300

Dimensions: Span (excluding winglets), 189 ft 2 in (57,66 m); length, 181 ft 7¼ in (55,35 m); height, 57 ft 7¾ in (17,57 m); wing area, 3,229 sq ft (300,00 m²).

ILYUSHIN IL-114

Country of Origin: USSR.

Type: Regional commercial transport.

Power Plant: Two 2,500 shp Isotov TV7-117 turboprops.

Performance: (Manufacturer's estimates) Max cruise speed, 311 mph (500 km/h) at 26,740 ft (8 150 m); optimum cruise altitude, 19,685–26,250 ft (6 000–8 000 m); range (with 11,905-lb/5 400-kg payload and reserves), 621 mls (1 000 km), (with 7,715-lb/3 500-kg payload and reserves), 1,770 mls (2 850 km), (with 3,307-lb/1 500-kg payload and reserves), 2,983 mls (4 800 km).

Weights: Operational empty, 30,204 lb (13 700 kg); max take-off, 46,296 lb (21 000 kg).

Accommodation: Flight crew of two and four-abreast seating for 60 passengers with central aisle.

Status: First prototype scheduled to enter flight test in June 1989, with production deliveries (to Aeroflot) commencing in 1991. Current planning calls for the manufacture of up to 500 Il-114s on three assembly lines during the 1990–95 five-year plan.

Notes: Possessing a close resemblance to the BAe ATP (see pages 54–55), the Il-114 has been designed as a successor to the Antonov An-24 on Aeroflot internal routes and is intended to operate from both paved and grass surfaces. The six-bladed propellers and the undercarriage are to be manufactured in Poland by WSK-PZL, and it is proposed that some other components be manufactured in various Comecon countries. An optional feature of the aircraft will be large carry-on baggage shelves in a lobby by the main door in the front of the cabin.

Dimensions: Span, 98 ft 5¼ in (30,00 m); length, 86 ft 3⅔ in (26,31 m); height, 30 ft 6⁹⁄₁₀ in (9,32 m).

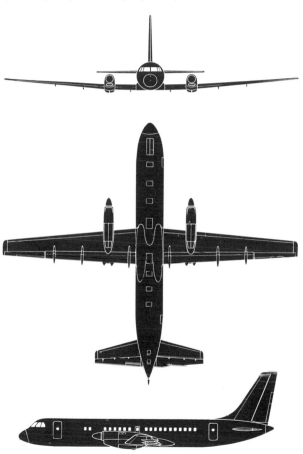

ILYUSHIN MAINSTAY

Country of Origin: USSR.
Type: Airborne early warning and control aircraft.
Power Plant: Four 26,455 lb st (12 000 kgp) Soloviev D-30KP turbofans.
Performance: (Estimated) Max cruise speed, 475 mph (764 km/h) at 29,500–42,650 ft (9 000–13 000 m); average loiter speed, 395 mph (636 km/h) at 29,500 ft (9 000 m); time on station (unrefuelled) at 930 mls (1 500 km) from base, 8–9 hrs.
Weights: (Estimated) Max take-off, 380,000 lb (172 370 kg).
Accommodation: Probable flight crew of four, with tactical and air direction teams totalling 9–12 personnel.
Status: An AEW&C derivative of the Il-76TD heavy duty transport and known to have been under test since 1979–80, Mainstay achieved initial operational capability in 1986, with 12–14 in service by beginning of 1989.
Notes: Serving with the Voyska PVO home defence force and tactical air forces, Mainstay is based on the Il-76TD from which externally it differs primarily in having a rotodome of (approx) 34 ft 6 in (10,50 m) diameter on twin pylons above the centre fuselage aft of the CG and large horizontal flat plate strakes on the aft part of the main undercarriage pods. The flight refuelling probe suggests that Mainstay is operated in conjunction with the Il-78 Midas tanker. The MiG-31 (see pages 162–3) is apparently optimised to operate with Mainstay which is also known to have operated with the Su-24 and Su-27.

ILYUSHIN MAINSTAY

Dimensions: Span, 165 ft 8½ in (50,50 m); length, 152 ft 10¼ in (46,59 m); height, 48 ft 5⅝ in (14,76 m); wing area, 3,229·2 sq ft (300,00 m²).

JAFFE AIRCRAFT SA-32T

Country of Origin: USA.

Type: Side-by-side two-seat basic trainer.

Power Plant: One 420 shp Allison 250-B17D turboprop.

Performance: (Estimated) Max speed, 332 mph (534 km/h) at sea level; normal cruise (75 per cent power), 316 mph (508 km/h); initial climb, 3,700 ft/min (18,8 m/sec); service ceiling, 25,000 ft (7 620 m); max range (no reserves), 1,105 mls (1 779 km).

Weights: Empty (typical), 1,560 lb (708 kg); max take-off, 2,600 lb (1 179 kg).

Status: Prototype SA-32T scheduled to enter flight test during the first quarter of 1989.

Notes: The SA-32T, designed by Edward J Swearingen, is a military instructional derivative of the SX300 high-performance two-seater, which, powered by a 300 hp Textron Lycoming IO-540 piston engine, established FAI-recognised international speed records in the C1c and C1b classes. The SA-32T utilises the same low-drag laminar-flow aerofoil, and will, it is claimed, simulate the flying behaviour of jet aircraft to which the pupil pilot will transition, with a consequent reduction in the number of instructional hours before conversion. Other features of the SA-32T also adhere to the philosophy that the pupil should be introduced to fighter-like handling at the earliest possible stage. The narrow-track undercarriage, for example, has been patterned on the landing gears of latest generation fighters and can be extended at jet approach speeds. The SA-32T is to be offered in kit form for assembly in Third World countries or as a total manufacturing package.

JAFFE AIRCRAFT SA-32T

Dimensions: Span, 24 ft 4⅘ in (7,44 m); length, 22 ft 6 in (6.86 m); height, 7 ft 9⅗ in (2,38 m); wing area, 71·5 sq ft (6,64 m²).

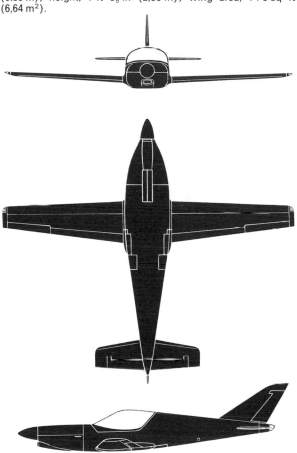

KAWASAKI T-4

Country of Origin: Japan.
Type: Tandem two-seat basic trainer.
Power Plant: Two 3,670 lb st (1 665 kgp) Ishikawajima Harima F3-IHI-30 turbofans.
Performance: Max speed (at 10,361 lb/4 700 kg), 616 mph (990 km/h) at 25,000 ft (7 620 m), or Mach=0·9, 645 mph (1 038 km/h); max initial climb, 10,000 ft/min (50,8 m/sec); range (at 12,125 lb/5 500 kg), 806 mls (1 297 km), (with two 99 Imp gal/450 1 drop tanks), 1,036 mls (1 668 km).
Weights: Empty, 8,157 lb (3 700 kg); normal loaded, 12,125 lb (5 500 kg); max take-off, 16,535 lb (7 500 kg).
Armament: (Weapons training) One 7,62-mm gun pod on centreline fuselage station and one AIM-9L Sidewinder AAM on each of two wing stations, or up to four 500-lb (227-kg) bombs.
Status: First of four XT-4 prototypes flown on 25 July 1985, with first production T-4 following on 28 June 1988. Orders placed for 52 T-4s of which deliveries scheduled for completion March 1991, with production tempo building up to two monthly at beginning of 1989. Further 22 called for in 1969 defence budget request, with total procurement for Air Self-Defence Force expected to exceed 200 aircraft.
Notes: The T-4 is intended to replace both the Lockheed T-33A and the Fuji T-1 in the training syllabus of Japan's Air Self-Defence Force, and has been developed jointly by Kawasaki (as prime contractor), Mitsubishi and Fuji. It is the first Japanese aircraft to combine a nationally-designed engine with an indigenous airframe for 25 years. The T-4 is to be phased into the instructional syllabus during the summer of 1989.

KAWASAKI T-4

Dimensions: Span, 32 ft 7½ in (9,94 m); length, 42 ft 8 in (13,00 m); height, 15 ft 1¼ in (4,60 m); wing area, 226·05 sq ft (21,00 m²).

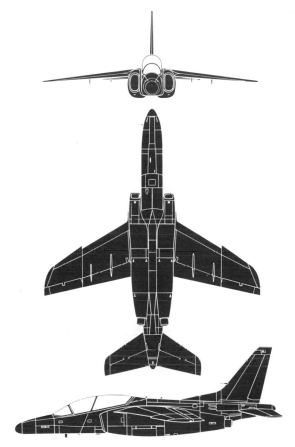

LET L-610

Country of Origin: Czechoslovakia.
Type: Short-haul regional transport.
Power Plant: Two 1,822 shp Motorlet M 602 turboprops.
Performance: (Manufacturer's estimates) Max cruise speed, 304 mph (480 km/h) at 23,620 ft (7 200 m); long-range cruise, 253 mph (408 km/h); max initial climb, 1,870 ft/min (9,5 m/sec); service ceiling, 33,630 ft (10 250 m); range (max payload and 45 min reserves), 540 mls (870 km), (max fuel) 1,495 mls (2 406 km).
Weights: Operational empty, 19,246 lb (8 730 kg); max take-off, 30,865 lb (14 000 kg).
Accommodation: Flight crew of two and standard arrangement for 40 passengers four abreast with central aisle.
Status: First of five prototypes flown 27 December 1988, with certification to Soviet standards to follow in 1990, and first customer deliveries (Aeroflot) late that year.
Notes: Designed for short-haul operations (stage lengths of 250–375 mls/400–600 km), the L-610 is claimed to offer better short landing and take-off capabilities than its closest western rivals. Intended to complement the smaller L-410 (of which Aeroflot operates some 600) and the larger Il-114 in Aeroflot's fleet (consideration was being given at the beginning of 1989 to the adaptation of the latter's 'glass' cockpit for the Let aircraft), the L-610 has been designed for soft field operation and for decent rates demanded by 'difficult' strips. A 48-passenger stretched version is projected.

Dimensions: Span, 84 ft 0 in (25,60 m); length, 70 ft 3¼ in (21,42 m); height, 24 ft 11½ in (7,61 m); wing area, 602·8 sq ft (56,00 m²).

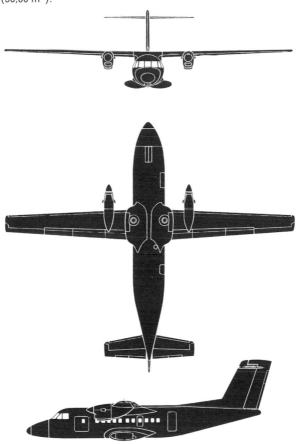

LOCKHEED F-117A

Country of Origin: USA.
Type: Single-seat low-altitude low-observable interdictor.
Power Plant: Two 10,800 lb st (4 900 kgp) General Electric F404 turbofans.
Performance: No details available at time of closing for press, but known to be subsonic.
Weights: No details available.
Armament: Missiles housed internally by two weapons bays.
Status: The F-117A flew for the first time in June 1981, and achieved initial operational capability in October 1983. A total of 59 F-117As has been ordered by the USAF of which 52 had been delivered by late 1988, and production being scheduled to terminate in 1990.
Notes: Designed to evade enemy radar and infrared detection, and conduct low-altitude strikes against high-priority targets, the F-117A possesses a unique multi-faceted shape to minimise radar returns and a special surface finish to absorb some radar energy. Together with a minimal radar cross section and the use of a low-level approach, probably using terrain masking, the F-117A can presumably get within weapons-release range of its target before detection. The three-view silhouette appearing on the opposite page should be considered as provisional, the planview depicting the upper surfaces of which more information is available. The fuselage of the F-117A appears almost tetrahedral, tapered front and rear, the flat surfaces adding to the aircraft's low-observable characteristics by reducing radar backscatter. The dorsal engine efflux nozzles enable the exhaust to be bled over the aft fuselage, thus screening heat emissions.

LOCKHEED F-117A

Dimensions: Estimated wingspan, 40 ft 0 in (12,20 m). No further details available.

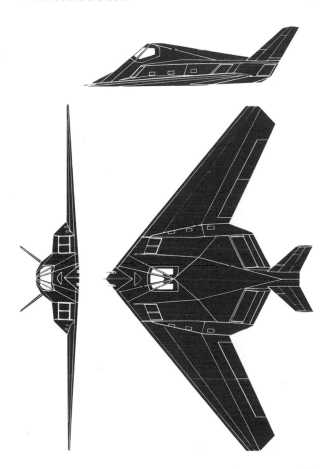

LOCKHEED L-100-30 HERCULES

Country of Origin: USA.
Type: Medium/long-haul military and commercial freighter.
Power Plant: Four 4,508 ehp Allison T56-A-15 turboprops.
Performance: Max cruise speed (at 120,000 lb/54 430 kg), 355 mph (571 km/h) at 20,000 ft (6 100 m); max initial climb, 1,700 ft/min (8,64 m/sec); range (with 51,054-lb/23 158-kg payload and 45 min reserves), 1,536 mls (2 472 km), (zero payload and 45 min reserves), 5,562 mls (8 950 km).
Weights: Operational empty, 77,736 lb (35 260 kg); max take-off, 155,000 lb (70 310 kg).
Accommodation: Normal flight crew of four and provision for 97 casualty stretchers plus medical attendants, 128 combat troops or 92 paratroopers. As a freighter a max payload of 51,054 lb (23 158 kg) may be carried. Loads including such heavy equipment as a 26,640-lb (12 080-kg) refuelling trailer or up to seven 463L freight pallets.
Status: A total of 1,900 Hercules (all versions) had been delivered by the beginning of 1989 (including some 110 commercial models) when production was continuing at an average of three aircraft monthly.
Notes: The L-100-30 and its military equivalent, the C-130H-30, are stretched versions of the basic Hercules, the C-130H. The original commercial model, the L-100-20, featured a 100-in (2,54-m) stretch over the basic military version, and the L-100-30, intended for both commercial and military applications, embodies a further 80-in (2,03-m) stretch. Military operators of the L-100-30 include Dubai, Ecuador, Gabon (illustrated above), Indonesia, Kuwait, Pakistan, Peru and the Philippines. Five of an airborne hospital version, the L-100-30HS, have been delivered to Saudi Arabia. The equivalent C-130H-30 serves with 11 air forces.

LOCKHEED L-100-30 HERCULES

Dimensions: Span, 132 ft 7 in (40,41 m); length, 112 ft 9 in (34,37 m); height, 38 ft 3 in (11,66 m); wing area, 1,745 sq ft (162,12 m²).

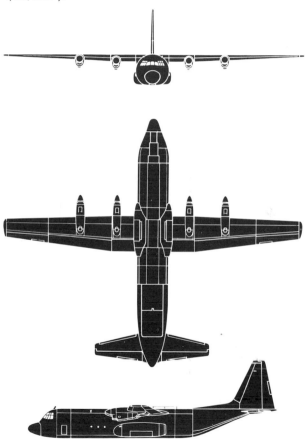

LOCKHEED P-3C ORION

Country of Origin: USA.

Type: Long-range maritime patrol aircraft.

Power Plant: Four 4,910 ehp Allison T56-A-14W turboprops.

Performance: Max speed (at 105,000 lb/47 625 kg), 473 mph (761 km/h) at 15,000 ft (4 570 m); econ cruise, 378 mph (608 km/h) at 25,000 ft (7 620 m); patrol speed, 237 mph (381 km/h) at 1,500 ft (457 m); max initial climb, 1,950 ft/min (9,9 m/sec); mission radius (three hours on station at 1,500 ft/ 457 m), 1,550 mls (2 494 km); max mission radius (no time on station at 135,000 lb/61 235 kg), 2,383 mls (3 835 km).

Weights: Empty, 61,491 lb (27 890 kg); normal loaded, 135,000 lb (61 235 kg); max overload take-off, 142,000 lb (64 410 kg).

Accommodation: Normal flight crew of 10 including five in tactical compartment.

Armament: Two Mk 101 depth charges and four Mk 43, 44 or 46 torpedoes, or eight Mk 54 bombs or eight torpedoes in weapons bay, and provision for up to 13,713 lb (6 220 kg) of ordnance on 10 stations.

Status: Prototype (YP-3C) flown 8 October 1968, with deliveries to the US Navy (in Update III form) terminating in 1989 with 287th P-3C. Other users of the P-3 (all versions) comprise Australia, Canada, Iran, Japan, Netherlands, New Zealand, Norway, Portugal and Spain. The P-3C followed 157 P-3As and 125 P-3Bs, and licence manufacture of the P-3C is continuing in Japan (Kawasaki) against requirement for 100.

Notes: Designated successor to the P-3 in US Navy service is a derivative, the LRAAWCA (Long Range Air Anti-submarine Warfare Capability Aircraft) for operation from 1995.

LOCKHEED P-3C ORION

Dimensions: Span, 99 ft 8 in (30,37 m); length, 116 ft 10 in (35,61 m); height, 33 ft 8½ in (10,29 m); wing area, 1,300 sq ft (120,77 m²).

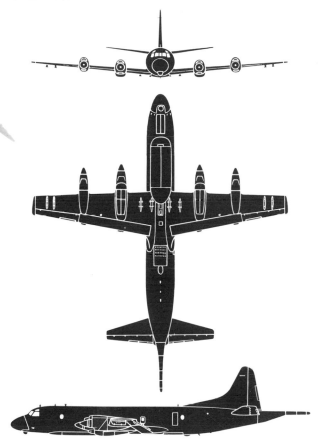

LOCKHEED P-3 SENTINEL

Country of Origin: USA.

Type: Airborne early warning and control aircraft.

Power Plant: Four 4,910 ehp Allison T56-A-14 turboprops.

Performance: Max cruise speed, 410 mph (660 km/h) at 15,000 ft (4 570 m); econ cruise, 373 mph (600 km/h) at 25,000 ft (7 620 m); average loiter speed, 310 mph (500 km/h); time on station (unrefuelled), 8·5 hrs at 920 mls (1 480 km) from base; max range, 4,836 mls (7 783 km); max endurance, 14 hrs.

Weights: Empty, 68,554 lb (31 096 km); max take-off, 139,760 lb (63 395 kg).

Accommodation: Flight crew of four and tactical team of four, plus provision for relief personnel or tactical team of 7–10 (according to equipment).

Status: Prototype (converted from P-3B) first flown on 13 June 1984, and flown with (APS-125) radar on 8 April 1988. Delivered to US Customs Service on 17 June 1988, this organisation holding options on three more at the beginning of 1989.

Notes: Derived from the P-3 Orion maritime patrol and ASW aircraft (see pages 142–3), the Sentinal is being proposed with various levels of equipment sophistication. The version for the US Customs Service, which is employed in the surveillance of drug-smuggling routes, is a comparatively simple aircraft with an APS-125 search radar and has a 24-ft (7,32-m) diameter APA-171 rotodome. For military operations, the Sentinel would be fitted with an APS-139 radar (as fitted to the E-2C Hawkeye), a C^3 system to receive, process and transmit tactical information and an AR-187 satellite communications system. This enhanced-capability version was being offered at the beginning of 1989 to various operators of the P-3 Orion.

LOCKHEED P-3 SENTINEL

Dimensions: Span, 99 ft 8 in (30,37 m); length, 107 ft $7\frac{1}{3}$ in (32,80 m); height, 33 ft $8\frac{1}{2}$ in (10,27 m); wing area, 1,300 sq ft (120,77 m²).

145

LTV YA-7F CORSAIR II

Country of Origin: USA.

Type: Single-seat attack and close air support aircraft.

Power Plant: One 14,370 lb st (6 518 kgp) dry and 23,450 lb st (10 637 kgp) Pratt & Whitney F100-PW-220 turbofan.

Performance: Max speed (without external stores), 803 mph (1 292 km/h) at 10,000 ft (3 050 m), or Mach = 1·1, (with six Mk 82 bombs), 737 mph (1 190 km/h) at sea level, or Mach = 0·967; time to 30,000 ft (9 150 m) with six Mk 82 bombs, 1·6 min; tactical radius (strike/interdiction mission on internal fuel with 6,000 lb/2 720 kg ordnance including 115-ml/185-km dash), 472 mls (760 km), (with two 250 Imp gal/1 135 l tanks retained), 690 mls (1 110 km).

Weights: Empty, 21,066 lb (9 555 kg); max take-off, 46,000 lb (20 865 kg).

Armament: One 20-mm rotary cannon and max external ordnance load of 17,380 lb (7 883 kg) distributed between two fuselage and six wing stores stations.

Status: First of two YA-7F prototypes (converted from A-7D airframes) scheduled to fly 10 April with second following in May 1989. Decision to undertake similar conversion of up to 337 Air National Guard A-7s for use as interim close air support aircraft scheduled to be taken in autumn of 1989.

Notes: Featuring an engine bay configured to take either the F100-PW-220 engine or the General Electric F110-GE-100, the YA-7F is an extensively upgraded rebuild of the 20-year-old baseline A-7D. Changes include a 47·5-in (1,20-m) fuselage stretch, the introduction of new augmented wing flaps and lift spoilers, and provision of a taller vertical tail. The YA-7F will incorporate LANA (Low Altitude Night Attack) equipment integrating Forward-Looking Infra-Red (FLIR), head-up display and navigation weapons delivery computer.

LTV YA-7F CORSAIR II

Dimensions: Span, 38 ft 9 in (11,80 m); length, 50 ft 1½ in (15,27 m); height, 16 ft 0¾ in (4,90 m); wing area, 375 sq ft (34,83 m²).

McDONNELL DOUGLAS F-15E EAGLE

Country of Origin: USA.

Type: Two-seat dual-role (air-air and air-ground) fighter.

Power Plant: Two 14,370 lb st (6 518 kgp) dry and 23,450 lb st (10 637 kgp) reheat Pratt & Whitney F100-PW-220 turbofans.

Performance: Max speed (short-endurance dash), 1,676 mph (2 698 km/h) at 40,000 ft (12 190 m), or Mach = 2·54, (sustained), 1,518 mph (2 443 km/h), or Mach = 2·3; service ceiling, 60,000 ft (18 300 m); ferry range (with conformal tanks and max external fuel), 3,570 mls (5 745 km).

Weights: Basic operational empty, 31,700 lb (14 379 kg); max take-off, 81,000 lb (36 741 kg).

Armament: One 20-mm six-barrel rotary cannon and (air-air) up to four each AIM-7 and AIM-9 AAMs, or up to eight AIM-120 AAMs, or (attack) up to 23,500 lb (10 659 kg) of ordnance on wing and fuselage stations plus tangential carriers.

Status: First production F-15E flown on 11 December 1986. USAF requirement for 392 of this dual-role version of the Eagle, with operational capability from 1989.

Notes: The F-15E has been derived from the basic Eagle (see 1986 edition) for long-range, deep interdiction and high-ordnance-load air-ground missions by day, night or in adverse weather. Embodying a restressed and strengthened structure affording double the life of earlier Eagles, the F-15E has engine bays tailored to accept either the F100 (as above) or the General Electric F110 engine. It has an APG-70 radar, upgraded mission computer and electronic warfare equipment, a programmable stores management system and a triplex digital (fly-by-wire) flight control system. The USAF has a requirement for 1,286 F-15s (of all versions), current production versions in addition to the F-15E being the single-seat F-15C air superiority fighter and its tandem two-seat operational training equivalent, the F-15D. Israel has received 51 F-15As, Bs and Cs, Saudi Arabia has procured 60 F-15Cs and Ds, and Japan plans purchase of 187 F-15Js and DJs (173 being licence-built).

McDONNELL DOUGLAS F-15E EAGLE

Dimensions: Span, 42 ft 9¾ in (13,05 m); length, 63 ft 9 in (19,43 m); height, 18 ft 5½ in (5,63 m); wing area, 608 sq ft (56,50 m²).

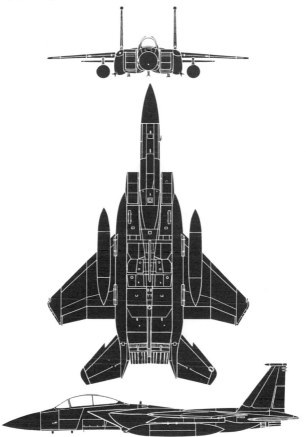

McDONNELL DOUGLAS F/A-18 HORNET

Country of Origin: USA.

Type: Single-seat shipboard and shore-based multi-role fighter and attack aircraft.

Power Plant: Two 10,600 lb st (4 810 kgp) dry and 15,800 lb st (7 167 kgp) reheat General Electric F404-GE-400 turbofans.

Performance: Max speed (AAMs on wingtip and fuselage stations), 1,190 mph (1 915 km/h) at 40,000 ft (12 150 m), or Mach = 1·8; max initial climb (half fuel and wingtip AAMs), 60,000 ft/min (304,6 m/sec); combat radius (air patrol), 480 mls (770 km), (with three 315 US gal/1 192 l external tanks), 735 mls (1 180 km).

Weights: Empty, 23,050 lb (10 455 kg); loaded (fighter mission), 36,710 lb (16 651 kg), (attack), 49,224 lb (22 238 kg); max take-off, 56,000 lb (25 400 kg).

Armament: One 20-mm rotary cannon and (air-air) two AIM-9 AAMs at wingtips and two AIM-7 AAMs on fuselage stations, or (attack) up to 17,000 lb (7 711 kg) between nine stations.

Status: First of 11 development aircraft flown 18 November 1978, with first production F/A-18A following in April 1980. Deliveries to US Navy of 410 (including two-seat F/A-18Bs) completed 1987 when supplanted by F/A-18C and D, first F/A-18C having flown 3 September 1987. Total anticipated US Navy procurement approximately 1,150 of which some 520 delivered by 1989 from production of 10 monthly of which three for export. Export orders comprise 114 CF-18As and 24 two-seat CF-18Bs for Canada, 57 AF-18As and 18 two-seat ATF-18As for Australia (licence-built by ASTA) and 60 EF-18As and 12 two-seat EF-18Bs for Spain.

Notes: Forty Hornets to be supplied to Kuwait, and upgraded version with 17,600 lb st (7 983 kgp) F404(EPA) engines to be procured by Switzerland (with initial contract for 34). Dedicated recce version, the RF-18D to be supplied to US Marine Corps (83) from 1990.

McDONNELL DOUGLAS F/A-18 HORNET

Dimensions: Span, 37 ft 6 in (11,43 m); length, 56 ft 0 in (17,07 m); height, 15 ft 4 in (4,67 m); wing area, 400 sq ft (37,16 m²).

McDONNELL DOUGLAS/BAE T-45A GOSHAWK

Country of Origin: USA (United Kingdom).
Type: Tandem two-seat carrier-capable basic/advanced trainer.
Power Plant: One 5,700 lb st (2 585 kgp) Rolls-Royce Turboméca F405-RR-400L (Adour Mk 861-49) turbofan.
Performance: Max speed, 620 mph (997 km/h) at 8,000 ft (2 440 m), 573 mph (922 km/h) at 30,000 ft (9 150 m), or Mach = 0·85; max initial climb, 6,982 ft/min (35,47 m/sec); time to 30,000 ft (9 150 m), 7·2 min; service ceiling, 42,250 ft (12 875 m); ferry range, (internal fuel), 1,150 mls (1 850 km), (with two 156 US gal/591 l external tanks), 1,819 mls (2 928 km).
Weights: Empty, 9,394 lb (4 261 kg); max take-off, 12,758 lb (5 787 kg).
Status: First of two pre-production T-45As flown on 16 April 1988. Thirty-six T-45As contracted for by beginning of 1989, with production deliveries scheduled to begin early 1990, with initial operational capability being attained September 1990. US Navy requirement for 302 T-45As with production peaking at 48 per year in 1993 and final deliveries in 1997.
Notes: Derived from the BAe Hawk (see pages 58–59), the T-45A Goshawk will be part of an integrated training system (T-45TS) embodying aircraft, academics, simulators and logistics support. Seventy-six per cent of the manufacture of the T-45A is being undertaken in the USA, and differences to the Hawk include addition of an arrester hook, relocation of the air brakes, revised undercarriage, changes to the wing movable surfaces and provision of catapult nose-tow launch assemblies. The T-45A is to replace the T-2C Buckeye and the TA-4J Skyhawk in the US Navy's training syllabus. The T-45TS is to provide ground and flight training for up to 600 carrier-qualified US Navy pilots annually, commencing in 1990.

McDONNELL DOUGLAS/BAE T-45A GOSHAWK

Dimensions: Span, 30 ft 9¾ in (9,39 m); length (including probe), 39 ft 3⅛ in (11,97 m); height, 13 ft 5 in (4,09 m); wing area, 179·64 sq ft (16,69 m²).

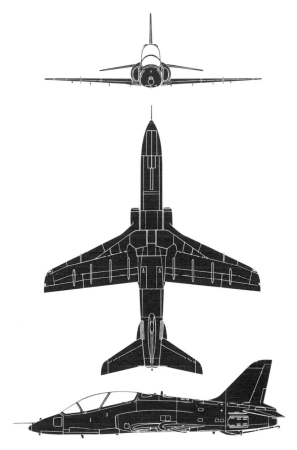

McDONNELL DOUGLAS MD-11

Country of Origin: USA.

Type: Medium/long-haul commercial transport.

Power Plant: Three 60,000 lb st (27 216 kgp) Pratt & Whitney PW4360, 61,500 lb st (27 896 kgp) General Electric CF6-80C2-D1F, or 65,000 lb st (29 484 kgp) Rolls-Royce RB211-524L turbofans.

Performance: (Manufacturer's estimates with PW4360) Max cruise speed (at 480,000 lb/217 728 kg), 580 mph (933 km/h) at 31,000 ft (9 450 m), or Mach=0·87; long-range cruise, 545 mph (877 km/h) at 31,000 ft (9 450 m), or Mach=0·818; max initial climb, 2,770 ft/min (14,07 m/sec); range (with max payload), 6,910 mls (11 120 km) at 546 mph (879 km/h) at 31,000 ft (9 450 m), (max fuel), 9,477 mls (15 250 km).

Weights: Operational empty, 277,300 lb (125 783 kg); max take-off, 602,500 lb (273 289 kg).

Accommodation: Flight crew of two and standard mixed-class seating for 323 passengers, with maximum of 405.

Status: First MD-11 was scheduled to enter flight test March 1989, with certification and initial customer deliveries anticipated second quarter 1990. A total of 88 orders, and 162 options and reserves was claimed at the beginning of 1989.

Notes: Derived from the DC-10, the MD-11 features a longer fuselage, aerodynamic improvements and an advanced two-crew all-digital flight deck, and makes extensive use of composite materials. Three versions are currently on offer: the baseline MD-11 airliner, a freighter version and a Combi capable of carrying 168–240 two-class passengers and 4–10 cargo pallets, depending on configuration. At the beginning of 1989, versions of the MD-11 under study included a standard-size aircraft with lower deck (forward of the wing) seating and a stretched version with a 35-ft (10,67-m) longer fuselage.

McDONNELL DOUGLAS MD-11

Dimensions: Span, 169 ft 6 in (51,66 m); length, 200 ft 10 in (61,21 m); height, 57 ft 9 in (17,60 m); wing area, 3,648 sq ft (338,90 m²).

McDONNELL DOUGLAS MD-87

Country of Origin: USA.

Type: Short/medium-haul commercial transport.

Power Plant: Two 20,860 lb st (9 462 kgp) Pratt & Whitney JT8D-217B/C turbofans.

Performance: Max cruise speed, 575 mph (925 km/h) at 27,000 ft (8 230 m); econ cruise, 522 mph (840 km/h) at 33,000 ft (10 060 m); long-range cruise, 505 mph (813 km/h) at 35,000 ft (10 670 m); range (max payload), 2,144 mls (3 450 km), (max fuel), 3,405 mls (5 480 km).

Weights: Operational empty, 73,157 lb (33 253 kg); max take-off, 140,000 lb (63 500 kg).

Accommodation: Flight crew of two and max single-class seating for 115–139 passengers five-abreast with optional mixed-class arrangements to suit customer requirements.

Status: First MD-87 flown on 4 December 1986, with first customer deliveries (to Austrian and Finnair) October 1987. Five hundred and sixty-eight MD-80 series aircraft delivered by beginning of 1989, when orders, options and reserves for all versions of the MD-80 series totalled 1,353 aircraft, with production continuing at approximately eight monthly.

Notes: The MD-80 series was developed from the DC-9 and is currently being offered in five versions, the MD-81, -82, -83 and -88 having a common fuselage length of 135 ft 6 in (41,30 m) and an overall length of 147 ft 10 in (45,06 m), and the MD-87 (described and illustrated) having a shorter fuselage. All versions have fundamentally the same wing, but differ in weight and power plant. The MD-80 family offers an example of new technology being applied retrospectively to an existing design (ie, the DC-9 which first flew in February 1965). The first MD-80 (initially the DC-9-80 and then the Super 80) was first flown on 18 October 1979. Twenty-five MD-82s are being co-manufactured by the Shanghai Aviation Industrial Corporation, the first of these being flown on 2 July 1987. The version of the MD-82 with an advanced cockpit is designated MD-88.

McDONNELL DOUGLAS MD-87

Dimensions: Span, 107 ft 10 in (32,85 m); length, 130 ft 5 in (39,75 m); height, 30 ft 6 in (9,30 m); wing area, 1,270 sq ft (117,98 m²).

McDONNELL DOUGLAS TAV-8B HARRIER II

Countries of Origin: USA and United Kingdom.
Type: Tandem two-seat conversion trainer.
Power Plant: One 21,450 lb st (9 730 kgp) Rolls-Royce F402-RR-406A vectored-thrust turbofan.
Performance: Max speed, 667 mph (1 074 km/h) at sea level, or Mach = 0·87, 587 mph at altitude, or Mach = 0·9 ; ferry range (with two 300 US gal/1 136 l external tanks retained), 1,647 mls (2 650 km).
Weights: Operational empty (including crew), 14,221 lb (6 451 kg); max take-off (for STO), 29,750 lb (13 495 kg).
Armament: Two twin-store wing stations for four LAU-68 rocket launchers or six Mk 76 practice bombs.
Status: First of multi-year purchases (1985–89) of 27 TAV-8Bs flown on 21 October 1986, with initial deliveries to the US Marine Corps following in August 1987.
Notes: A two-seat operational training version of the AV-8B single-seat close support aircraft (which also serves with the RAF as the Harrier GR Mk 5 – see pages 56–57 – and the Spanish Navy as the EAV-8B Matador II), the TAV-8B has been developed by McDonnell Douglas with British Aerospace as sub-contractor. It features a new two-seat forward fuselage and new vertical tail, but is in other respects similar to the single-seater. The US Marine Corps has a requirement for 304 AV-8Bs, the first of five pilot production aircraft having flown on 29 August 1983, and procurement of 276 (including TAV-8Bs) had been approved by the beginning of 1989. With delivery of the 167th aircraft a night attack system has been incorporated, this including a FLIR (Forward-Looking Infra-Red) system, a prototype of this version having flown on 26 June 1987. Aircraft delivered from 1990 are to have the uprated F402-RR-408 engine of approx 24,500 lb st (11 113 kgp).

McDONNELL DOUGLAS TAV-8B HARRIER II

Dimensions: Span, 30 ft 4 in (9,24 m); length, 50 ft 3 in (15,32 m); height, 13 ft 4¾ in (4,08 m); wing area (including LERX), 238·7 sq ft (22,18 m²).

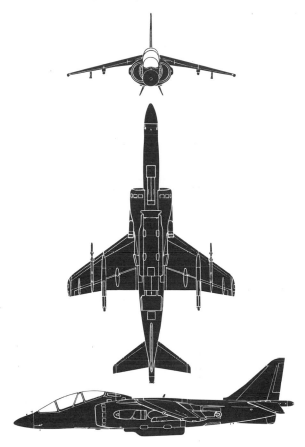

MIKOYAN MIG-29 (FULCRUM)

Country of Origin: USSR.
Type: Single-seat counterair fighter.
Power Plant: Two 11,243 lb st (5 100 kgp) dry and 18,300 lb st (8 300 kgp) reheat Tumansky RD-33 turbofans.
Performance: Max speed (four AAMs and 75 per cent internal fuel), 1,518 mph (2 445 km/h) at 36,100 ft (11 000 m), or Mach = 2·3, 915 mph (1,470 km/h) at sea level, or Mach = 1·2; initial climb, 64,960 ft/min (330 m/sec); service ceiling, 55,775 ft (17 000 m); combat radius (subsonic area intercept with 330 Imp gal/1 500 l centreline tank and four AAMs), 630 mls (1 015 km); max range, 1,305 mls (2 100 km).
Weights: Max take-off (approx), 39,683 lb (18 000 kg).
Armament: One 30-mm cannon, plus four AA-10 Alamo A/C semi-active radar-guided and Alamo-B IR-homing medium-range and two AA-11 Archer close-combat IR missiles. (Secondary ground attack) Bombs, 16- or 32-round 57-mm or 20-round 80-mm pods, or 240-mm S-24 rockets on six wing stations.
Status: First prototype flown 1977, with initial service deliveries 1983. Some 700 delivered by beginning of 1989, with production continuing at four factories (Moscow, Kuybyshev and Ulianovsk). Deliveries 1987–88 to India, Iraq, North Korea, Syria and Yugoslavia, the first WarPac recipient being East Germany.
Notes: The initial production series of the MiG-29 are the single-seat *Fulcrum-A* (described and illustrated above and opposite) and the two-seat *Fulcrum-B*, or MiG-29UB (*Uchebny Boyevoi*, or Combat Trainer). The latter lacks the coherent multi-mode pulse-Doppler radar, known to NATO as *Slot Back*. A further version, *Fulcrum-C*, features an enlarged fuselage dorsal to increase internal fuel capacity. Negotiations have been conducted for licence manufacture of the MiG-29 by Hindustan Aeronautics in India.

MIKOYAN MIG-29 (FULCRUM)

Dimensions: Span, 37 ft 4½ in (11,36 m); length, 56 ft 9⅞ in (17,32 m); height, 15 ft 3 in (4,73 m); wing area, 409·04 sq ft (38,00 m²).

MIKOYAN MIG-31 (FOXHOUND)

Country of Origin: USSR.

Type: Tandem two-seat all-weather interceptor.

Power Plant: Two 30,865 lb st (14 000 kgp) reheat Tumansky R-31F turbojets.

Performance: (Estimated) Max speed, 1,520 mph (2 445 km/h) above 36,100 ft (11 000 m), or Mach = 2·3; max combat radius (area intercept mission with four AA-9 Amos and two AA-8 Aphid AAMs), 1,180 mls (1 900 km); ceiling, 80 000 ft (24 385 m).

Weights: (Estimated) Empty equipped, 47,000 lb (21 320 kg); normal loaded, 65,000–70,000 lb (29 485–31 750 kg); max take-off, 88,185 lb (40 000 kg).

Armament: Eight AA-9 Amos semi-active radar-homing long-range AAMs (four in tandem pairs on fuselage centreline and four paired on two wing pylons), or four AA-9 Amos and four AA-8 Aphid close-combat IR-homing AAMs.

Status: The MiG-31 was developed from the mid 'seventies and was first deployed by the Voyska PVO air defence forces from early 1983. In excess of 200 believed in service by the beginning of 1989, with production continuing at Gorkiy.

Notes: While fundamentally based on the MiG-25 of the late 'sixties, the design of the MiG-31 is largely new. Possessing accommodation for a pilot and weapon systems operator in tandem, the MiG-31 has a lookdown/shootdown pulse-Doppler weapons system and multiple-target engagement capability. An unusual feature is the staggered tandem arrangement of the main wheels so that weight during take-off and landing is spread over a larger surface area. Retention by the MiG-31 of the arc-welded nickel steel structure of the MiG-25 has not been confirmed, but the better heat-resistant properties of steel are unnecessary at the MiG-31's speeds.

MIKOYAN MIG-31 (FOXHOUND)

Dimensions: (Estimated) Span, 45 ft 9 in (13,94 m); length (excluding probe), 68 ft 10 in (21,00 m); height, 18 ft 6 in (5,63 m); wing area, 602·8 sq ft (56,00 m²).

NORTHROP B-2

Country of Origin: USA.

Type: Two-seat low-observable multi-role bomber.

Power Plant: Four 19,000 lb st (8 620 kgp) class General Electric F118-GE-100 turbofans.

Performance: (Estimated) Max speed, 595–628 mph (955 1 010 km/h) at 50,000 ft (15 240 m), or Mach = 0·9–0·95, 570 mph (917 km/h) at sea level, or Mach = 0·75; max unrefuelled range, 8,050 mls (12 955 km).

Weights: Estimated max take-off, 300,000 lb (136 080 kg).

Armament: Approx max of 75,000 lb (34 000 kg) of ordnance accommodated by three internal bays each of which may be fitted with an eight-round rotary launcher for medium-range cruise missiles.

Status: First B-2 was scheduled to enter flight test early in 1989, with six aircraft (all built on production tooling) to participate in test programme, five of these later being configured for operational use. The USAF has a requirement for 132 B-2s of which 120 will be nuclear capable, with first deliveries in Fiscal 1991, and initial operational capability 1992–3.

Notes: The B-2 advanced technology bomber possesses low observable characteristics and is intended for both high- and low-altitude penetration to attack both fixed and mobile targets. Its structure is primarily of carbonfibre and Kevlar, with some titanium employed in high-stress areas, and extensive use is made of radar-absorbent composite skinning. The two-dimensional efflux nozzles of the engines exhaust over the inboard trailing edges of the thick supercritical wing to screen heat emissions, and the aircraft is of relaxed-stability design with a fly-by-wire flight control system. The head-on radar cross section of the B-2 is allegedly one-tenth of that of the B-1B, and all external features are designed to present the smallest radar, electro-optical and infrared signatures possible when viewed from any aspect. The planview drawing (opposite) depicts the upper surfaces as all details of the underside were classified at the time of closing for press.

NORTHROP B-2

Dimensions: (Approximate) Span, 172 ft (52,42 m); length, 69 ft (21,03 m); height, 17 ft (5,18 m).

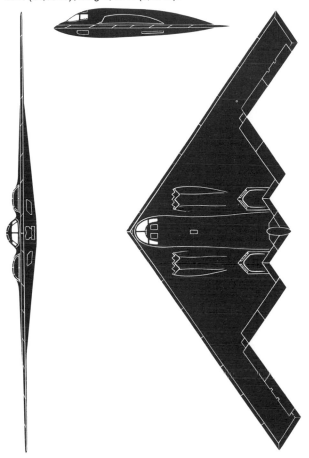

OMAC LASER 300

Country of Origin: USA.
Type: Light business executive transport.
Power Plant: One 750 shp Pratt & Whitney Canada PT6A-135A turboprop.
Performance: (Manufacturer's estimates) Max cruise speed, 291 mph (468 km/h) at 25,000 ft (7 620 m); econ cruise, 230 mph (370 km/h); max initial climb, 2,010 ft/min (10,21 m/sec); service ceiling, 30,000 ft (9 150 m); range (with max payload), 1,610 mls (2 591 km), (with max fuel), 2 412 mls (3 882 km).
Weights: Empty, 5,100 lb (2 313 kg); max take-off, 8,350 lb (3 787 kg).
Accommodation: Pilot and co-pilot/passenger on flight deck and standard seating in main cabin for five passengers in two single seats and on one three-seat divan. Club seating arrangements and a high-density layout for eight passengers are options.
Status: First production Laser 300 flown on 29 July 1988, with FAA certification and first customer deliveries anticipated for second quarter of 1989.
Notes: Derived from the OMAC I prototype which first flew on 11 December 1981, and embodying numerous design changes, the Laser 300 is of innovative canard configuration, an unusual feature being its over-cabin strake fuel tanks. Of fail-safe fatigue-resistant design, the Laser 300 is of conventional light metal semi-monocoque construction.

Dimensions: Span, 41 ft 6 in (12,65 m); length, 29 ft 7 in (9,02 m); height, 9 ft 10 in (3,00 m); wing area, 260 sq ft (24,15 m²).

PANAVIA TORNADO F MK 3

Country of Origin: United Kingdom.
Type: Tandem two-seat air defence fighter.
Power Plant: Two (approx) 9,000 lb st (4 082 kgp) dry and 17,000 lb st (7 711 kgp) reheat Turbo-Union RB199-34R Mk 104 turbofans.
Performance: (Estimated) Max speed, 920 mph (1 480 km/h) at sea level, or Mach = 1·2, 1,450 mph (2 333 km/h) at 40,000 ft (12 190 m), or Mach = 2·2; time to 30,000 ft (9 145 m), 1·7 min; tactical radius (combat air patrol with two 330 Imp gal/1 500 l drop tanks and allowance for 2 hrs loiter), 350–450 mls (560–725 km); ferry range (with four 330 Imp gal/1 500 l external tanks), 2,650 mls (4 265 km).
Weights: (Estimated) Empty equipped, 31,970 lb (14 500 kg); normal loaded (four Sky Flash and four AIM-9L AAMs) 50,700 lb (30 000 kg); max take-off, 56,000 lb (25 400 kg).
Armament: One 27-mm cannon plus four each Sky Flash and AIM-9L AAMs.
Status: First of three F Mk 2 prototypes flown on 27 October 1979, and first of 18 production F Mk 2s (including six F Mk 2Ts) flown 5 March 1984. Production subsequently converted to F Mk 3 of which deliveries commenced July 1986 after initial flight on 20 November 1985. Orders for the F Mk 3 for the RAF (including F Mk 2s) comprise 165 aircraft, plus 15 as attrition replacements, and essentially similar aircraft are being supplied to Saudi Arabia (60) and Oman (8).
Notes: The Tornado F Mk 3 is the definitive air defence version for the RAF of the multi-national (UK, Federal Germany and Italy) interdictor strike (IDS) aircraft. The air defence version (ADV) possesses some 80 per cent commonality with the IDS aircraft. An electronic combat and reconnaissance version of the IDS is being developed for the Luftwaffe.

Dimensions: Span (25 deg sweep), 45 ft $7\frac{1}{4}$ in (13,90 m), (68 deg sweep), 28 ft $2\frac{1}{2}$ in (8,59 m); length, 59 ft $3\frac{7}{8}$ in (18,08 m); height, 18 ft $8\frac{1}{2}$ in (5,70 m); wing area, 322·9 sq ft (30,00 m²).

PIAGGIO P.180 AVANTI

Country of Origin: Italy.

Type: Light corporate transport.

Power Plant: Two 850 shp Pratt & Whitney Canada PT6A-66 turboprops.

Performance: (Manufacturer's estimates) Max cruise speed, 460 mph (740 km/h) at 27,000 ft (8 230 m); econ cruise, 368 mph (593 km/h) at 41,000 ft (12 495 m); max initial climb, 3,650 ft/min (18,54 m/sec); certificated operational ceiling, 41,000 ft (12 495 m); range (with four passengers and IFR reserves), 2,072 mls (3 335 km) at econ cruise.

Weights: Operational empty, 6,900 lb (3 130 kg); max take-off, 10,510 lb (4 767 kg).

Accommodation: Pilot and co-pilot/passenger on flight deck with standard main cabin configuration for seven passengers in individual seats and optional arrangements for 5–9 passengers.

Status: Two prototypes flown on 23 September 1986 and 15 May 1987, with the first series aircraft scheduled to follow mid 1989, and certification anticipated at the end of 1989, customer deliveries commencing early 1990.

Notes: The Avanti is highly innovative in configuration, being of so-called 'three-surface' concept, a foreplane balancing an aft-located mainplane and a tailplane being retained for pitch control. This arrangement is claimed to result in significant aerodynamic benefits. The wing is of laminar flow section and high aspect ratio, and novel constructional methods are employed to provide an exceptionally smooth outer skin. The Avanti is primarily of metal construction, but composite parts include the foreplane, tail surfaces, engine nacelles, nose cone and some wing elements. The entire fuselage back to the rear pressure bulkhead and including the cockpit is being built at Wichita from where it is shipped to Italy for final assembly.

PIAGGIO P.180 AVANTI

Dimensions: Span, 45 ft 4⅞ in (13,84 m); length, 46 ft 5⅞ in (14,17 m); height, 12 ft 9½ in (3,90 m); wing area, 169·64 sq ft (15,76 m²).

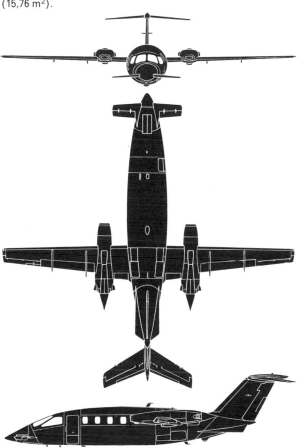

PILATUS PC-9

Country of Origin: Switzerland.

Type: Tandem two-seat basic/advanced trainer.

Power Plant: One 950 shp Pratt & Whitney Canada PT6A-62 turboprop.

Performance: (At 4,960 lb/2 250 kg) Max speed, 311 mph (500 km/h) at sea level, 345 mph (556 km/h) at 20,000 ft (6 100 m); max initial climb, 4,100 ft/min (20,83 m/sec); max range (five per cent fuel reserve plus 20 min), 1,020 mls (1 642 km) at 25,000 ft (7 620 m).

Weights: Basic empty, 3,715 lb (1 685 kg); max take-off (aerobatic), 4,960 lb (2 250 kg), (utility), 7,055 lb (3 200 kg).

Status: First and second prototypes flown on 7 May and 20 July 1984, with first production deliveries (against an order for four from Burma) late 1985. Subsequent deliveries include 30 for Saudi Arabia, 15 for Iraq and four for Angola. Sixty-seven have been ordered by the RAAF of which two were supplied flyaway by the parent company, 17 have been supplied as kits for assembly by Hawker de Havilland, and the remaining 48 are to be built by the Australian company. An initial batch of four (against eventual requirement of 12–16) was in process of delivery to the Swiss Air Force at the beginning of 1989.

Notes: Despite a close external resemblance to the lower-powered PC-7 (see 1984 edition), the PC-9 is a very different aircraft, possessing only some 10 per cent structural commonality with the earlier trainer. Those PC-9s being supplied to the Swiss Air Force are equipped for target towing and target presentation duties, and the PC-9s delivered to Saudi Arabia have cockpit instrumentation closely compatible with that of the BAe Hawk which has also been procured by that country.

PILATUS PC-9

Dimensions: Span, 33 ft 2½ in (10,12 m); length, 33 ft 4¾ in (10,17 m); height, 10 ft 8⅓ in (3,26 m); wing area, 175·3 sq ft (16,29 m²).

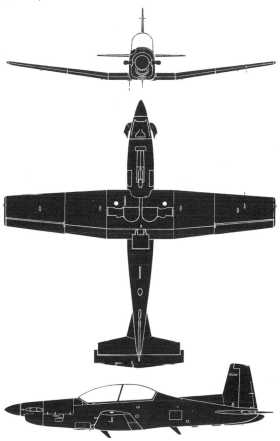

PROMAVIA JET SQUALUS F 1300

Country of Origin: Belgium (Italy).
Type: Side-by-side two-seat primary/basic trainer.
Power Plant: One 1,330 lb st (603 kgp) Garrett TFE109-1 turbofan.
Performance: (Manufacturer's estimates) Max speed, 345 mph (556 km/h); max initial climb, 3,200 ft/min (16,25 m/sec); service ceiling, 37,000 ft (11 280 m); ferry range (max internal fuel), 1,150 mls (1 853 km) at 20,000 ft (6 095 m).
Weights: Empty equipped, 2,866 lb (1 300 kg); loaded (aerobatic), 4,410 lb (2 000 kg); max take-off, 5,291 lb (2 400 kg).
Armament: (F 1500) Provision for four wing stores stations with a maximum external load of 1,323 lb (600 kg). Typical proposed loads include two 12,7-mm, 20-mm or double 7,62-mm gun pods, four seven-round 2·75-in (70-mm) rocket pods, or four 250-lb (113,4-kg) bombs.
Status: First of two prototypes flown 30 April 1987, with second prototype scheduled to fly early 1989 and FAR Part 23 certification anticipated by mid 1989.
Notes: With series production projected to commence in Belgium by Sonaca SA on behalf of Promavia SA during 1990, the Jet Squalus (Shark) has been designed by Stelio Frati of the Italian General Avia concern, the prototypes having been built in Italy. The first prototype is expected to be re-engined with a TFE109 uprated to 1,500 lb st (680 kgp) during 1989 to meet USAF (to which the Jet Squalus is being offered) performance requirements. The second prototype is to be equipped for civil airline training, and a third aircraft will be completed to full USAF specifications, including cockpit pressurisation, complete environmental control and lighter ejection seats.

PROMAVIA JET SQUALUS F 1300

Dimensions: Span, 29 ft $7\frac{7}{8}$ in (9,04 m); length, 30 ft $8\frac{1}{2}$ in (9,36 m); height, 11 ft $9\frac{3}{4}$ in (3,60 m); wing area, 146·18 sq ft (13,58 m²).

PZL MIELEC M-26 ISKIERKA

Country of Origin: Poland.

Type: Tandem two-seat primary/basic trainer.

Power Plant: One (M-26 00) 205 hp PZL-F 6A-350CA or (M-26 01) 300 hp Textron Lycoming AEIO-540-L1B5D six-cylinder horizontally-opposed engine.

Performance: (M-26 01) Max speed, 211 mph (340 km/h) at sea level; max initial climb, 1,575 ft/min (8,0 m/sec); max range (with 30 min reserves), 1,007 mls (1 620 km).

Weights: Operational empty, 2,072 lb (940 kg); max take-off, 3,086 lb (1 400 kg).

Status: First prototype (M-26 00) flown on 15 July 1986, with second prototype (M-26 01) following on 24 June 1987. No production plans announced by beginning of 1989.

Notes: The Iskierka (Little Spark) has been developed by PZL Mielec to FAR Part 23 airworthiness requirements and is intended for the training of civil pilots and for pilot selection for military training, and is seen as complementary to the WSK-PZL Warszawa-Okecie-produced PZL-130 Orlik (see pages 178–9). The Iskierka embodies some components of the M-20 Mewa (Gull), a PZL version of the Piper PA-34 Seneca II six/seven-seat executive transport and ambulance aircraft, notably in the wings, tail assembly, undercarriage, and electrical and power systems, and is being developed with both the indigenously-manufactured PZL-F 6A (licence-manufactured Franklin) and Textron Lycoming IO-540 flat-six engines. It is currently being proposed as a successor to the PZL-110 Koliber (licence-built version of the Socata Rallye 100 ST) as the principal tuitional aircraft of the Aero Club of the Polish People's Republic, and the higher-powered Lycoming-engined version is to be aimed primarily at the export market.

PZL MIELEC M-26 ISKIERKA

Dimensions: Span, 28 ft 2⅔ in (8,60 m); length, 27 ft 2¾ in (8,30 m); height, 9 ft 8½ in (2,96 m); wing area, 150·7 sq ft (14,00 m²).

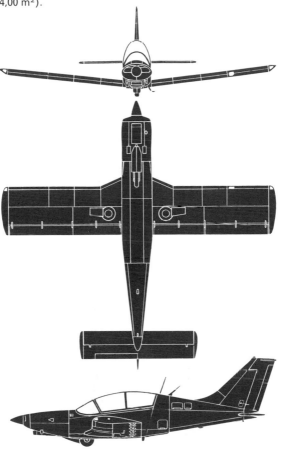

PZL-130 ORLIK

Country of Origin: Poland.
Type: Tandem two-seat primary/basic trainer.
Power Plant: One 330 hp Vedeneyev M-14Pm nine-cylinder radial air-cooled engine.
Performance: (At 3,196 lb/1 450 kg) Max speed, 211 mph (340 km/h); max cruise (75% power), 180 mph (290 km/h); max initial climb, 1,378 ft/min (7,0 m/sec); service ceiling, 14,000 ft (4 270 m); range (with max fuel and no reserves), 880 mls (1 416 km) at 143 mph (230 km/h), (utility), 793 mls (1 276 km) at 105 mph (170 km/h).
Weights: Empty equipped, 2,529 lb (1 147 kg); max take-off (aerobatic), 3,196 lb (1 450 kg), (utility), 3,527 lb (1 600 kg).
Armament: (Weapons training) Four wing stores stations for practice bombs, guns or rocket pods, inboard stations stressed for 441 lb (200 kg) and outboard stations for 353 lb (160 kg).
Status: First of three flying prototypes flown 12 October 1984, and second on 29 December 1984. Construction of pre-series aircraft commenced 1986, with deliveries from late 1987.
Notes: Third flying prototype adapted to take 550 shp Pratt & Whitney Canada PT6A-25A turboprop as Turbo Orlik in which form it first flew on 13 July 1986. This aircraft was subsequently destroyed (see 1988 edition). The Orlik is intended for service with the Polish Air Force, and a noteworthy feature is its low aspect ratio wing.

PZL-130 ORLIK

Dimensions: Span, 26 ft 3 in (8,00 m); length, 27 ft 8¾ in (8,45 m); height, 11 ft 7 in (3,53 m); wing area, 132·18 sq ft (12,28 m²).

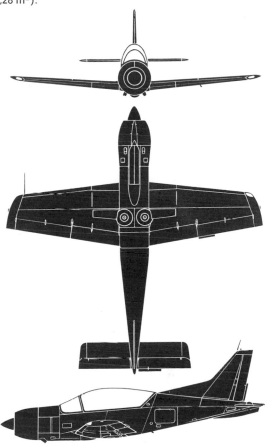

ROCKWELL B-1B

Country of Origin: USA.

Type: Strategic bomber and cruise missile carrier.

Power Plant: Four 30,780 lb st (13 960 kgp) General Electric F101-GE-102 turbofans.

Performance: Max speed (without external ordnance), 795 mph (1 280 km/h) above 36,000 ft (10,975 m), or Mach= 1·25; low-level penetration speed, 610 mph (980 km/h), or Mach=0·8; approx unrefuelled range, 7,500 mls (12 070 km).

Weights: Empty, 184,300 lb (83 500 kg); empty equipped, 192,000 lb (87 090 kg); max take-off, 477,000 lb (216 367 kg).

Accommodation: Flight crew of four comprising pilot, co-pilot/navigator, and defensive and offensive systems operators.

Armament: Three fuselage weapons bays to accommodate up to 84 500-lb (227-kg) Mk 82 bombs, 24 2,000-lb (908-kg) Mk 84 bombs or 2,439-lb (1 106-kg) B-83 nuclear bombs, or eight AGM-86B cruise missiles plus 12 AGM-69 defence suppression missiles. Up to 44 Mk 82 bombs or 14 720-lb (327-kg) B-61 nuclear bombs, or 14 AGM-86B missiles on six external stores stations beneath fuselage.

Status: First of 100 production B-1Bs flown on 18 October 1984, with initial deliveries to the USAF commencing on 29 June 1985, and final aircraft delivered on 30 April 1988.

Notes: The B-1B is an extensively revised derivative of the B-1A, the first of four prototypes of which first flew on 23 December 1974, two of these subsequently being converted to B-1B standards. By comparison with the B-1A, the B-1B has fixed engine air intakes, uses radar absorbent material in certain areas of the airframe and offers a reduced radar signature. During the summer of 1987, the B-1B established a series of international speed and distance with payload records, including a 3,107-mile (5 000-km) closed-circuit with a 66,140-lb (30 000-kg) payload at 655 mph (1 054 km/h).

ROCKWELL B-1B

Dimensions: Span (15 deg sweep), 136 ft 8½ in (41,67 m), (67·5 deg sweep), 78 ft 2½ in (23,84 m); length, 147 ft 0 in (44,81 m); height, 34 ft 0 in (10,36 m); wing area (approx), 1,950 sq ft (181,20 m²).

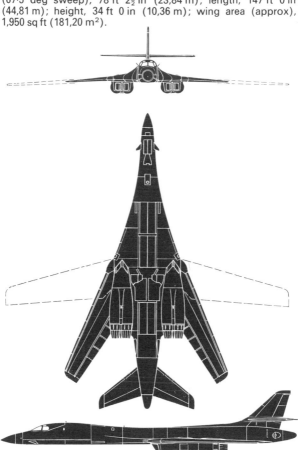

ROCKWELL/MBB X-31A

Countries of Origin: USA and Federal Germany.
Type: Fighter manoeuvrability demonstration aircraft.
Power Plant: One 10,600 lb st (4 808 kgp) General Electric F404-GE-400 turbofan.
Performance: Max speed, 598 mph (962 km/h) at 35,000 ft (10 670 m), or Mach = 0·9.
Weights: Empty, 10,212 lb (4 632 kg); design mission, 11,830 lb (5 366 kg); max take-off, 13,968 lb (6 335 kg).
Status: First of two flight demonstrators scheduled to commence flight test programme in November 1989.
Notes: The first of the US X-series aircraft to be developed jointly with another country, the X-31A is intended as a research tool for use in the EFM (Enhanced Fighter Manoeuvrability) programme. The participating companies are Rockwell International of the USA and Messerschmitt-Bölkow-Blohm of Federal Germany, and the X-31A is being funded jointly by the US (75 per cent) and German (25 per cent) governments. Featuring a cranked delta wing and canard surfaces, the X-31A is intended to integrate several technologies, including vectored thrust and integrated control systems, to expand the manoeuvring flight envelope. The results of the EFM programme are expected to provide a future generation of fighter aircraft with new tactical capabilities by capitalising on all-aspect weapons for air combat and by high agility, both above and below conventional stall limits. The X-31A is expected to be able to fly at angles of attack in excess of 60 deg before stalling, as compared with up to 35 deg for current fighters, and its turning circle radius will be between one-third and one-half of that of present-generation aircraft. The flight test programme will be conducted by an international team from the US Navy and the Federal German Luftwaffe.

Dimensions: Span, 23 ft 10 in (7,26 m); length (excluding probe), 43 ft 2 in (13,21 m); height, 14 ft 7 in (4,44 m); wing area, 226·3 sq ft (21,02 m²).

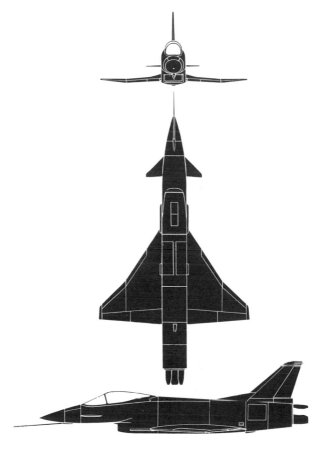

SAAB 39 GRIPEN

Country of Origin: Sweden.

Type: Single-seat multi-role fighter.

Power Plant: One 12,250 lb st (5 510 kgp) dry and 18,100 lb st (8 210 kgp) General Electric/Volvo RM 12 turbofan.

Performance: No details available at the time of closing for press, but maximum speed is expected to range from 914 mph (1 470 km/h) at sea level, or Mach = 1·2, to 1,450 mph (2 555 km/h) above 36,000 ft (10 975 m), Mach = 2·2.

Weights: Approx clean loaded, 17,635 lb (8 000 kg).

Armament: One 27-mm Mauser BK 27 cannon and (intercept) four Rb 72 Sky Flash and two Rb 24 Sidewinder AAMs, or (attack mission) various electro-optically guided ASMs, area weapons or RBS 15F anti-shipping missiles on wing stations.

Status: First of five prototypes was flown on 9 December 1988, with four additional prototypes scheduled to join the flight test programme during the course of 1989–90. Initial contract placed June 1982 for 30 aircraft with an option on a further 110 aircraft up to the year 2000. First deliveries to the Swedish Air Force scheduled for 1992–93, and total Air Force requirement for 340–400 aircraft.

Notes: The Gripen (Griffon), or JAS 39, has been designed to fulfil fighter, attack and reconnaissance roles, all necessary hardware and software for the three tasks being carried permanently, mission changes calling only for the provision of the appropriate external stores. The Gripen makes extensive use of composites in its fail-safe construction – more than 30 per cent of the fuselage is of composite material – and features a triple-redundant digital fly-by-wire flight control system. Although no official requirement has been announced for a tandem-two-seat conversion training version of the Gripen, a design study had been completed by the beginning of 1989 of the two-seat JAS 39B incorporating a 1·64-ft (0,5-m) fuselage plug for the second cockpit.

SAAB 39 GRIPEN

Dimensions: (Approximate) Span, 26 ft 3 in (8,00 m); length, 46 ft 3 in (14,00 m); height, 15 ft 5 in (4,70 m).

SAAB 340

Country of Origin: Sweden.
Type: Regional commercial and corporate transport.
Power Plant: Two (340A) 1,735 shp General Electric CT7-5A2, or (340B) 1,870 shp CT7-9B turboprops.
Performance: (340A) Max cruise speed (at 26,000 lb/ 11 793 kg), 313 mph (504 km/h) at 15,000 ft (4 575 m); range cruise, 288 mph (463 km/h) at 25,000 ft (7 620 m); max initial climb, 1,800 ft/min (9,14 m/sec); service ceiling, 25,000 ft (7 620 m); range (35 passengers and 45 min reserves), 725 mls (1 167 km) at range cruise, (30 passengers), 1,082 mls (1 742 km).
Weights: (340A) Typical operational empty, 17,415 lb (7 899 kg); max take-off, 28,000 lb (12 700 kg), (340B), 28,500 lb (12 927 kg).
Accommodation: Flight crew of two and standard regional airline arrangement for 35 passengers three abreast.
Status: First of three prototypes flown on 25 January 1983, with 134 delivered and 153 ordered by beginning of 1989. Saab 340B scheduled to be certificated mid-1989 with initial customer deliveries (to Crossair) following in latter part of year.
Notes: The 340B features uprated engines and a longer-span tailplane, an extended CG envelope permitting greater payloads. At the beginning of 1989, a version for up to 50 passengers, the Saab 2000, had been launched, this having a 13% increase in wing area and a 20·34-ft (6,20-m) stretch. The prototype 340B is a conversion of the second prototype 340A.

SAAB 340

Dimensions: Span, 70 ft 4 in (21,44 m); length, 64 ft 8½ in (19,72 m); height, 22 ft 6 in (6,86 m); wing area, 450 sq ft (41,81 m²).

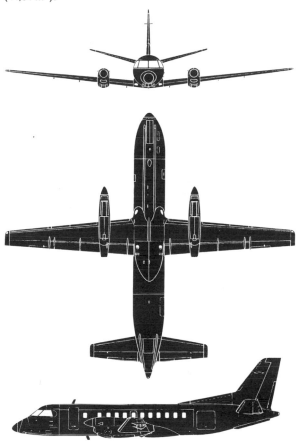

SAC (SHENYANG) J-8 II (FINBACK-B)

Country of Origin: China.

Type: Single-seat multi-role fighter.

Power Plant: Two 9,590 lb st (4 350 kgp) dry and 14,815 lb st (6 720 kgp) reheat LNAEF (Liyang) WP-13 turbojets.

Performance: Max speed, 1,452 mph (2 337 km/h) above 36,000 ft (10 975 m), or Mach = 2·2; max initial climb, 39,370 ft/min (200 m/sec); service ceiling, 65,620 ft (20 000 m); combat radius (with centreline drop tank and four AAMs for area intercept mission), 497 mls (800 km); max range (max external fuel), 1,367 mls (2 200 km).

Weights: Empty, 21,649 lb (9 820 kg); normal loaded, 31,525 lb (14 300 kg); max take-off, 39,242 lb (17 800 kg).

Armament: One 23-mm twin-barrel cannon and (intercept mission) up to six PL-2B infra-red dogfight, PL-4 radar-guided long-range or PL-7 semi-active radar medium-range AAMs, or (close air support) up to 8,818 lb (4 000 kg) of ordnance between one fuselage centreline and six wing stations.

Status: First of three J-8 II prototypes flown May 1984, with initial service introduction September 1988. Two being delivered to the USA early 1989 for flight test and certification of equipment upgrade package.

Notes: Fifty shipsets (plus five spare kits) of upgraded avionics suite comprising fire control radar, inertial navigation system, head-up display, air data computers and databus to be supplied to SAC (Shenyang Aircraft Co) during 1991–95 for installation in J-8 II fighters (the westernised designation being F-8 II).

Dimensions: Span, 30 ft 7⅞ in (9,34 m); length, 70 ft 10 in (21,59 m); height, 17 ft 9 in (5,41 m); wing area, 454·25 sq ft (42,20 m²).

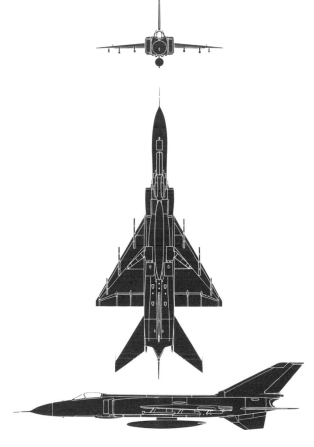

SHORTS (C-23A) SHERPA

Country of Origin: United Kingdom.
Type: Light freighter and utility aircraft.
Power Plant: Two 1,198 shp Pratt & Whitney Canada PT6A-45R turboprops.
Performance: Max cruise speed (at 21,000 lb/9 525 kg), 218 mph (352 km/h) at 10,000 ft (3 050 m); econ cruise, 181 mph (291 km/h); max initial climb, 1,180 ft/min (5,99 m/sec); range (7,000-lb/3 175-kg payload and 45 min reserves), 225 mls (362 km), (5,000-lb/2 268-kg payload), 770 mls (1 239 km).
Weights: Empty, 14,208 lb (6 445 kg); max take-off, 22,900 lb (10 387 kg).
Accommodation: Crew of two on flight deck and (in all-cargo configuration) accommodation for up to four LD3 or seven CO8 containers, with max payload of up to 7,000 lb (3 175 kg). Typical loads can comprise nine personnel and two LD3 containers, or (using load spreaders) two half-ton vehicles in the Land-Rover class.
Status: The prototype Sherpa was first flown on 23 December 1982, and the first of 18 ordered by the USAF to fulfil its EDSA (European Distribution System Aircraft) requirement as the C-23A was flown on 6 August 1984, with final delivery on 6 December 1985. Ten additional aircraft ordered by US Department of Defense in 1988 for use as light freighters by the National Guard. One has been supplied to Venezuela for a civil role, and the USAF holds options (until November 1990) on a further 48 aircraft.
Notes: The Sherpa is a freighter version of the Shorts 330–200 30-passenger commercial transport, retaining many features of the all-passenger model to permit utility passenger transport operations. The Sherpa's design incorporates a full-width rear cargo door/ramp which, actuated hydraulically, permits through loading.

SHORTS (C-23A) SHERPA

Dimensions: Span, 74 ft 8 in (22,76 m); length, 58 ft 0½ in (17,69 m); height, 16 ft 3 in (4,95 m); wing area, 453 sq ft (42,10 m²).

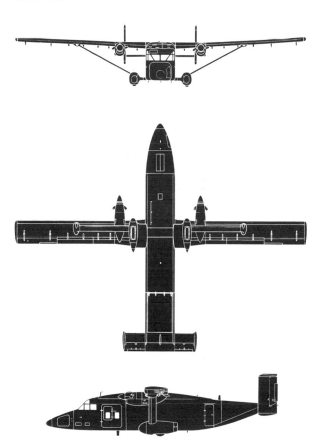

SHORTS 360-300

Country of Origin: United Kingdom.
Type: Regional commercial transport.
Power Plant: Two 1,424 shp Pratt & Whitney Canada PT6A-67R turboprops.
Performance: Max cruise speed (at 25,000 lb/11 340 kg), 249 mph (400 km/h) at 10,000 ft (3 050 m); range cruise, 207 mph (333 km/h); max climb, 952 ft/min (4,86 m/sec); range (with 36 passengers and reserves), 463 mls (745 km) at 249 mph (400 km/h), 732 mls (1 178 km) at 207 mph (333 km/h).
Weights: Operational empty (typical), 17,350 lb (7 870 kg); max take-off, 27,100 lb (12 292 kg).
Accommodation: Flight crew of two with all-passenger cabin arrangements for 36–39 seats, and optional all freight (360-300F) version with payload up to 10,000 lb (4 536 kg).
Status: Prototype (360) flown on 1 June 1981, with first production aircraft flying on 19 August 1982, and customer deliveries (Suburban Airlines) commencing in following December. The 360-300 introduced early 1987, with customer deliveries (to Philippine Airlines) commencing on 18 March 1987. Orders totalled 160 aircraft at beginning of 1989, with 145 delivered and 18 to be built in 1989.
Notes: The -300 version of the Shorts 360 is an upgraded version of the preceding production model, the Shorts 360 Advanced, with PT6A-67R turboprops replacing the -65R, improved passenger comfort and substantially reduced noise levels. The basic 360 is a growth version of the 330, differing primarily in having a 3-ft (91-cm) cabin stretch ahead of the wing and entirely redesigned rear fuselage and tail assembly. The fuselage stretch permitted the insertion of either two or three additional three-seat rows in the main cabin. It also resulted in reduced aerodynamic drag by comparison with the earlier aircraft.

SHORTS 360-300

Dimensions: Span, 74 ft 9½ in (22,80 m); length, 70 ft 9⅞ in (21,58 m); height, 23 ft 10¼ in (7,27 m); wing area, 454 sq ft (42,18 m²).

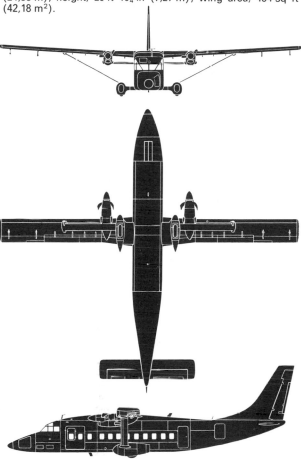

SHORTS S312 TUCANO MK 1

Country of Origin: United Kingdom (Brazil).
Type: Tandem two-seat basic trainer.
Power Plant: One 1,100 shp Garrett TPE331-12B turboprop.
Performance: Max speed (at 5,952 lb/2 700 kg), 315 mph (507 km/h) at 10,000–15,000 ft (3 050–4 575 m); econ cruise, 253 mph (407 km/h) at 20,000 ft (6 100 m); max initial climb, 3,510 ft/min (17,38 m/sec); service ceiling, 34,000 ft (10 365 m); max range (internal fuel), 1,035 mls (1 665 km) at 25,000 ft (7 620 m); tactical radius (weapons training mission at 7,220 lb/ 3 275 kg with 1,000 lb/454 kg of ordnance), 495 mls (797 km).
Weights: Empty equipped, 4,614 lb (2 093 kg); max take-off (aerobatic), 5,953 lb (2 700 kg), (weapons training), 7,264 lb (3 295 kg).
Armament: (Training and light attack) Wide range of podded weapons and underwing ordnance up to 2,000 lb (910 kg) distributed between four wing stations.
Status: Brazilian-built prototype flown on 14 February 1986, with first Shorts-built aircraft following on 30 December. Deliveries to RAF commenced on 16 June 1988, with formal service entry on 1 September. One hundred and thirty ordered for RAF, with production to attain four monthly during 1989. Fifteen ordered for Kenya Air Force.
Notes: Derived from the EMB-312 Tucano (see pages 98–99) specifically to meet an RAF requirement, the S312 Tucano T Mk 1 has a more powerful engine, structural strengthening to extend the fatigue life, a ventral airbrake and a revised cockpit layout. In RAF service, the Tucano T Mk 1 is replacing the Jet Provost in the tuitional syllabus, pilots then progressing to Hawks for advanced instruction and weapons training. The UK Ministry of Defence has an option on 15 additional aircraft.

SHORTS S312 TUCANO MK 1

Dimensions: Span, 37 ft 0 in (11,28 m); length, 32 ft 4¼ in (9,86 m); height, 11 ft 1⅞ in (3,40 m); wing area, 208·07 sq ft (19,33 m²).

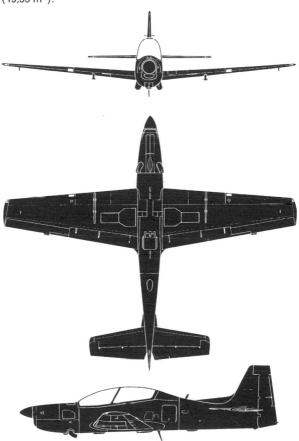

SIAI MARCHETTI S.211

Country of Origin: Italy.

Type: Tandem two-seat basic trainer.

Power Plant: One 2,500 lb st (1 134 kgp) Pratt & Whitney Canada JT15D-4D turbofan.

Performance: Max cruise speed, 414 mph (667 km/h) at 25,000 ft (7 620 m); range cruise, 311 mph (500 km/h) at 30,000 ft (9 150 m); max initial climb, 4,200 ft/min (21,34 m/sec); service ceiling, 40,000 ft (12 200 m); max range (internal fuel with 30 min reserves), 1,036 mls (1 668 km); ferry range (with two 77 Imp gal/350 l external tanks), 1,543 mls (2 483 km).

Weights: Empty equipped, 4,078 lb (1 850 kg); max take-off (training mission), 6,063 lb (2 750 kg), (with armament), 6,944 lb (3 150 kg).

Armament: (Weapons training and light attack) Maximum external ordnance load of 1,320 lb (600 kg) between four wing stations.

Status: First of three prototypes flown 10 April 1981, and first production aircraft (for Singapore) flown on 4 October 1984. First six for Singapore delivered as CKD kits for local assembly, with further 23 built by SAMCO. Four each to Uganda and Haiti, and 18 (with option on further 18) ordered by Philippine Air Force with delivery in CKD form during 1989–90 for assembly by Philippines Aerospace Development Corporation.

Notes: A lightweight, low-cost basic trainer and light attack aircraft, the S.211 is being offered with more advanced avionics and an uprated engine and lengthened fuselage. A firm decision to proceed with this enhanced version was still awaited at the beginning of 1989.

Dimensions: Span, 27 ft 8 in (8,43 m); length, 30 ft 6½ in (9,31 m); height, 12 ft 5½ in (3,80 m); wing area, 135·63 sq ft (12,60 m²).

SIAI MARCHETTI SF 600TP CANGURO

Country of Origin: Italy.
Type: Light utility transport.
Power Plant: Two 420 shp Allison 250-B17C turboprops.
Performance: Max cruise speed, 190 mph (306 km/h) at 5,000 ft (1 525 m); cruise (75% power), 178 mph (287 km/h) at 10,000 ft (3 050 m); max initial climb, 1,480 ft/min (7,52 m/sec); service ceiling, 24,000 ft (7 315 m); range (with max payload and reserves), 372 mls (600 km), (with max fuel and 1,102-lb/500-kg payload), 981 mls (1 580 km).
Weights: Empty (standard utility), 4,133 lb (1 875 kg); max take-off, 7,495 lb (3 400 kg).
Accommodation: Pilot and co-pilot/passenger on flight deck and various optional arrangements for up to nine passengers or six in corporate executive version. Medevac arrangement for two casualty stretchers and two medical attendants, and military transport version for 10 paratroops on inward-facing seats.
Status: SF 600TP first flown on 8 April 1981, followed by two additional prototypes of which second featured retractable undercarriage. First customer deliveries (three to Sun Line) mid 1988, and licence manufacture expected to be undertaken in Philippines (initially from CKD kits).
Notes: The SF 600TP Canguro (Kangaroo) is available with both fixed and retractable undercarriage, the former being the standard series version. It is being offered for a variety of missions, ranging from agricultural spraying and dusting with external tank or hopper to coastal surveillance with 360 deg ventral radar.

SIAI MARCHETTI SF 600TP CANGURO

Dimensions: Span, 49 ft $2\frac{1}{2}$ in (15,00 m); length, 39 ft $10\frac{1}{2}$ in (12,15 m); height, 15 ft 1 in (4,60 m); wing area, 258.3 sq ft (24,00 m²).

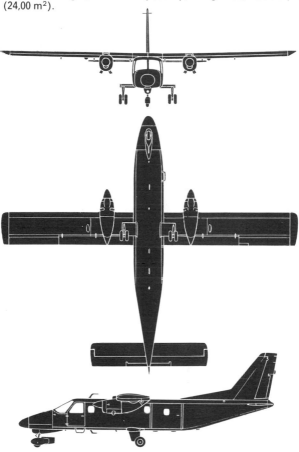

SUKHOI SU-24 (FENCER)

Country of Origin: USSR.

Type: Two-seat deep penetration interdictor and strike, reconnaissance and electronic warfare aircraft.

Power Plant: Two (Fencer-C) 17,675 lb st (8 020 kgp) dry and 25,350 lb st (11 500 kgp) reheat Tumansky R-29B turbojets.

Performance: (Estimated) Max sustained speed (without external stores), 1,440 mph (2 317 km/h) above 36,090 ft (11 000 m), or Mach = 2.·18, 915 mph (1 470 km/h) at sea level, or Mach = 1·2; tactical radius (with 6,615-lb/3 000-kg warload and two 660 Imp gal/3 000 1 drop tanks and HI-LO-LO-HI mission profile), 930 mls (1 500 km).

Weights: (Estimated) Empty equipped, 41,890 lb (19 000 kg); max take-off, 85,000–90,000 lb (38 560–40 800 kg).

Armament: One 30-mm six-barrel rotary cannon and up to (approx) 13,230 lb (6 000 kg) or ordnance on four fuselage and four wing stations, including such missiles as AS-7 Kerry, AS-10 Karen, AS-11 Kilter, AS-12 Kegler, AS-13 Kingbolt and AS-14 Kedge.

Status: Both fixed- and variable-geometry prototypes believed first flown 1969–70, with initial operational status achieved from late 1974. More than 800 (including 500 assigned to strategic missions) estimated in service with SovAF at beginning of 1989, and small quantities with Soviet Navy.

Notes: The Su-24 has been deployed in several versions, the most recent of these being a reconnaissance variant (referred to by NATO as Fencer-E and operated by Soviet Naval Aviation) and an electronic warfare version. Illustrated above and right is the Fencer-D, which, introduced in 1983, is currently the most widely-used version. The Su-24 has four wing sweep angle settings (16, 45, 55 and 68 deg) and is crewed by a pilot and weapon systems operator.

Dimensions: (Estimated) Span (16 deg sweep), 56 ft 6 in (17,25 m), (68 deg sweep), 33 ft 9 in (10,30 m); length (excluding probe), 72 ft 2 in (22,00 m); height, 18 ft 0 in (5,50 m).

SUKHOI SU-25 (FROGFOOT)

Country of Origin: USSR.

Type: Single-seat attack and close air support aircraft.

Power Plant: Two 9,340 lb st (4 237 kgp) Tumansky R-13-300 turbojets.

Performance: (Estimated) Max speed (without external stores), 528 mph (850 km/h) at 10,000 ft (3 050 m); combat radius (HI-LO-HI with 4,410 lb/2 000 kg of ordnance and two external fuel tanks and allowance for loiter), 340 mls (546 km); ferry range (max external fuel), 1,500 mls (2 414 km).

Weights: Empty, 20,950 lb (9 500 kg); normal loaded, 37,478 lb (17 000 kg); max take-off, 41,890 lb (19 000 kg).

Armament: One twin-barrel 30-mm cannon, two AA-8 Aphid self-defence AAMs and up to 8,820 lb (4 000 kg) ordnance distributed between eight of the 10 wing stations, including 16- or 32-round 57-mm rocket pods, 20-round 80-mm rocket pods, 240-mm S-240 rocket missiles, 1,100-lb (500-kg) retarded cluster bombs, etc.

Status: Prototypes of the Su-25 are believed to have flown during 1977–78, with initial deliveries to the SovAF commencing 1981–82. Some 300 delivered from Tbilisi facility at beginning of 1989, when production was continuing for the SovAF and for export. Export customers include Czechoslovakia, Hungary, Iraq and North Korea.

Notes: Employed from 1982 by the SovAF in Afghanistan, the Su-25 is broadly comparable with the USAF's A-10A Thunderbolt II and is suitable for operation from semi-prepared runways. Low-altitude manoeuvrability is aided by symmetrically- or differentially-operated split wingtip spoilers.

SUKHOI SU-25 (FROGFOOT)

Dimensions: (Estimated) Span, 46 ft 7 in (14,20 m); length (including nose probes), 49 ft 10½ in (15,20 m); height 15 ft 9 in (4,80 m); wing area, 362·75 sq ft (33,70 m²).

SUKHOI SU-27 (FLANKER-B)

Country of Origin: USSR.
Type: Single-seat counterair fighter.
Power Plant: Two (approx) 20,000 lb st (9 070 kgp) dry and 30,000 lb st (13 610 kgp) reheat Lyulka RD-32 turbofans.
Performance: (Estimated) Max speed, 1,518 mph (2 445 km/h) above 36,100 ft (11 000 m), or Mach = 2·3, 835 mph (1 345 km/h) at sea level, or Mach = 1·1; tactical radius (subsonic intercept mission with external fuel on centreline and six AAMs), 930 mls (1 500 km).
Weights: (Estimated) Normal loaded (air-air mission), 50,000 lb (22 675 kg); max take-off, 63,500 lb (28 800 kg).
Armament: One 30-mm six-barrel rotary cannon and up to 10 air-to-air missiles, a typical mix comprising six AA-10 Alamo-A, -B and -C medium-range missiles and four AA-11 Archer dogfight missiles.
Status: Prototype (T-10) flown in May 1977, with small pre-series (Flanker-A) for evaluation being followed by initiation of series production 1982–83 at Komsomolsk and initial deployment in 1986. Some 150 believed in service by beginning of 1989.
Notes: Possessing track-while-scan radar, a pulse-Doppler lookdown/shootdown weapon system, infrared search and tracking, and a digital data link, the series (Flanker-B) Su-27 differs in a number of respects from the prototype (T-10) and pre-series (Flanker-A) aircraft. Configurational differences include squared-off wingtips, repositioned and redesigned vertical tail surfaces, the introduction of ventral fins, a length-ened rear fuselage and aft-positioned nosewheel. An Su-27 (referred to as the P-42), established several time-to-altitude records in November–December 1986. These included 25·4 sec to 9,840 ft (3 000 m), 47.1 sec to 29,530 ft (9 000 m) and 58·14 sec to 39,370 ft (12 000 m).

SUKHOI SU-27 (FLANKER-B)

Dimensions: (Estimated) Span, 48 ft 3 in (14,70 m); length (excluding probe), 70 ft 10 in (21,60 m); height, 18 ft 0 in (5,50 m); wing area, 680 sq ft (63,20 m²).

TBM INTERNATIONAL TBM 700

Countries of Origin: France, USA and Finland.
Type: Light business and executive transport.
Power Plant: One 700 shp Pratt & Whitney Canada PT6A-40/1 turboprop.
Performance: (Manufacturer's estimates) Max cruise speed, 345 mph (556 km/h) at 25,000 ft (7 620 m); range cruise, 288 mph (463 km/h); max initial climb, 2,300 ft/min (11,7 m/sec); range with 45 min reserves (three occupants), 1,785 mls (2 870 km) at max cruise, 2,300 mls (3 705 km) at range cruise, (six occupants), 1,325 mls (2 130 km) at max cruise, 1,610 mls (2 590 km) at range cruise.
Weights: Empty, 3,290 lb (1 492 kg); max take-off, 5,890 lb (2 672 kg).
Accommodation: Pilot and co-pilot/passenger side-by-side on flight deck and up to six passengers in main cabin. Typical arrangement for four passengers with club seating and central aisle. Cabin fully pressurised.
Status: First of three prototypes flown on 14 July 1988, with FAR 23 certification anticipated by late 1989, initial production deliveries following early 1990.
Notes: The TBM 700 is being developed by the Aérospatiale subsidiary Socata in France, Mooney in the USA and Valmet in Finland, each consortium partner building specific parts for final assembly lines in France and the USA. The TBM 700 adopts the configuration of the pressurised Mooney M301 flown in 1983, the Aérospatiale input being primarily concerned with the wing. The rear fuselage and wing are to be manufactured by Mooney, Valmet producing the fin and tailplane, and the remainder will be built by Socata. Customers have been announced in France, West Germany and Sweden, and a market for some 600 aircraft is envisaged by the mid 'nineties.

TBM INTERNATIONAL TBM 700

Dimensions: Span, 39 ft 10¾ in (12,16 m); length, 34 ft 2½ in (10,43 m); height, 13 ft 1 in (3,99 m).

TUPOLEV TU-26 (BACKFIRE-C)

Country of Origin: USSR.

Type: Medium-range strategic bomber and maritime strike/reconnaissance aircraft.

Power Plant: Two (estimated) 35,000 lb st (15 875 kgp) dry and 50,000 lb st (22 680 kgp) reheat Kuznetsov turbofans.

Performance: (Estimated) Max speed (short-period dash), 1,320 mph (2 124 km/h) at 39,370 ft (12 000 m), or Mach = 2.0, (sustained), 1,090 mph (1 755 km/h), or Mach = 1.65; combat radius (unrefuelled high-altitude subsonic mission profile), 2,160 mls (4 200 km).

Weights: (Estimated) Max take-off, 285,000 lb (129 275 kg).

Armament: Remotely-controlled twin-barrel 23-mm cannon in tail barbette. Max internal load of free fall bombs and mines up to 26,460 lb (12 000 kg), or one (on fuselage centreline) or two (on wing centre section) AS-4 Kitchen inertially-guided stand-off missiles, plus AS-9 Kyle anti-radar missiles.

Status: The Backfire-C is the latest identified version of the Tu-26 (alias Tu-22M) and first appeared in service during 1985, but dedicated reconnaissance and electronic warfare versions are also in development/service. In excess of 400 Backfire-B and -C versions in service with SovAF and SovNav at beginning of 1989, some 150 of these with the latter, and production continuing at 30 per year.

Notes: The Backfire-C differs from the-B externally primarily in having larger, wedge-type air intakes to cater for more powerful engines.

TUPOLEV TU-26 (BACKFIRE-C)

Dimensions: (Estimated) Span (20 dag sweep), 112 ft 6 in (34,30 m), (65 deg sweep), 76 ft 9 in (23,40 m); length, 130 ft 0 in (39,62 m); wing area, 1,800 sq ft (167,22 m²).

TUPOLEV TU-160 (BLACKJACK-A)

Country of Origin: USSR.

Type: Long-range strategic bomber and maritime strike/reconnaissance aircraft.

Power Plant: Four (approx) 35,000 lb st (15 875 kgp) dry and 50,000 lb st (22 680 kgp) reheat Soloviev turbofans.

Performance: Max (over-target dash) speed, 1,518 mph (2 443 km/h) at 40,000 ft (12 200 m), or Mach = 2·3; range cruise, 595 mph (960 km/h) at 45,000 ft (13 720 m), or Mach = 0·9; unrefuelled combat radius (subsonic cruise, supersonic high-altitude dash and transonic low-altitude penetration), 4,540 mls (7 300 km).

Weights: (Estimated) Operational empty, 253,530 lb (115 000 kg); max take-off, 590,000 lb (267 625 kg).

Armament: Primary weapon is 1,850-mile (3 000-km) range AS-15 Kent subsonic low-altitude cruise missile (six carried in each of two weapons bays) or BL-10 supersonic short-range attack missile (12 in each bay), but provision is made for free-fall bombs or mix of bombs and missiles up to estimated maximum of 36,000 lb (16 330 kg).

Status: First seen under test at Ramenskoye, near Moscow, in 1979, the Tu-160 entered production at Kazan in 1984–85, initial operational capability being attained during 1988, with some 18 delivered by beginning of 1989, when production tempo was 1·0–1·5 aircraft monthly. This is expected to peak at 2·5 aircraft monthly in 1990.

Notes: Some 20 per cent larger than the Rockwell B-1B, the Tu-160 is initially replacing the Tu-95 Bear-A and supplementing the Tu-142 Bear-H in the Soviet strategic bombing force.

TUPOLEV TU-160 (BLACKJACK-A)

Dimensions: (Estimated) Span (20 deg sweep), 182 ft 0 in
(55,5 m), (65 dep sweep), 120 ft 6 in (36,75 m); length, 177 ft
0 in (53,95 m).

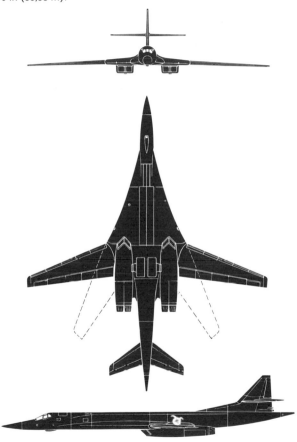

TUPOLEV TU-204

Country of Origin: USSR.
Type: Medium-haul commercial transport.
Power Plant: Two 35,300 lb st (16 000 kgp) Soloviev PS-90A turbofans.
Performance: (Manufacturer's estimates) Max speed, 559 mph (900 km/h); max continuous cruise, 528 mph (850 km/h) at 40,025 ft (12 200 m); econ cruise, 503 mph (810 km/h) at 34,940 ft (10 650 m); time (at 206,128 lb/93 500 kg) to 34,940 ft (10 650 m), 22 min, to 40,025 ft (12 200 m), 25 min; range (with max payload), 1,490 mls (2 400 km), (with 38,580-lb/17 500-kg payload), 2,175 mls (3 500 km), (with 29,760-lb/13 500-kg payload), 2,855 mls (4 600 km).
Weights: Empty, 124,559 lb (56 500 kg); max take-off, 206,128 lb (93 500 kg).
Accommodation: Flight crew of two (with option of three) with 214 passengers three abreast with central aisle and typical mixed-class arrangement for 12 first class, 47 business class and 111 tourist class passengers.
Status: First prototype Tu-204 flown on 2 January 1989, with customer deliveries commencing 1991 to Aeroflot (which has a requirement for 80–90 up to 1995), CSA and other Comecon airlines.
Notes: The Tu-204 is a narrow-body, medium-haul transport in the same general category as the Boeing 757, and makes extensive use of new materials in its construction, including composites, to achieve a low specific structural weight. The wing is of supercritical section, and triple inertial navigation systems are installed.

TUPOLEV TU-204

Dimensions: Span (over winglets), 137 ft $9\frac{1}{2}$ in (42,00 m); length, 150 ft 11 in (46,00 m); height, 45 ft $7\frac{1}{4}$ in (13,90 m).

VALMET L-90 TP REDIGO

Country of Origin: Finland.

Type: Side-by-side two-seat primary/basic trainer.

Power Plant: One 360 shp Allison 250 B17D turboprop.

Performance: Max speed, 208 mph (335 km/h) at 5,000 ft (1 525 m); cruise (75% power), 190 mph (305 km/h) at 9,840 ft (3 000 m); max initial climb, 1,930 ft/min (9,80 m/sec); time to 16,405 ft (5 000 m), 11·5 min; max range, 1,070 mls (1 725 km); endurance, 5·0 hrs.

Weights: Basic empty, 1,960 lb (889 kg); max take-off (aerobatic), 2,980 lb (1 352 kg), (normal), 3,530 lb (1 601 kg), (utility with external load), 4,190 lb (1 900 kg).

Armament: (Weapons training and light strike) Max external load of 1,764 lb (800 kg) distributed between six wing stations, typical loads (when flown as a single-seater) including four 330·5-lb (150-kg) bombs or two 551-lb (250-kg) bombs, plus two flare pods.

Status: The Allison-powered first prototype Redigo was flown in July 1986, with a second prototype powered by a Turboméca TP.319 turboprop flown on 3 December 1987. The latter was lost in an accident on 29 August 1988. The Finnish government placed, on 6 January 1989, a contract for an initial batch of 10 Allison-powered Redigos for delivery in 1991–92 and for use in the liaison role.

Notes: Derived from the piston-engined L-70 Vinka via the L-80 TP (see 1986 edition), the L-90 Redigo utilises the same basic fuselage as its predecessors, and is being offered with either the Allison 250-B17D or Turboméca TM.319 turboprop. One of the lightest of the current generation of turboprop-powered trainers, the Redigo is fully aerobatic and is stressed for plus 7 *g* and minus 3·5 *g*.

VALMET L-90 TP REDIGO

Dimensions: Span, 33 ft 11 in (10,34 m); length, 25 ft 11 in (7,90 m); height, 9 ft $4\frac{1}{4}$ in (2,85 m); wing area, 158·77 sq ft (14,75 m²).

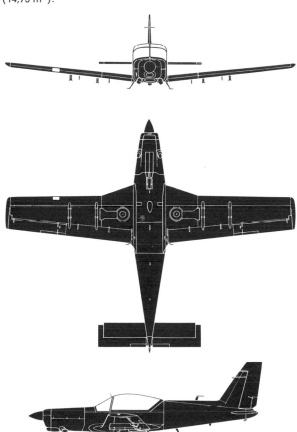

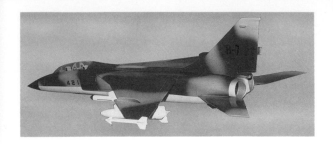

XAC (XIAN) H-7

Country of Origin: China.
Type: Two-seat interdictor and anti-shipping strike aircraft.
Power Plant: (Prototypes) Two 12,250 lb st (5 550 kgp) dry and 20,525 lb st (9 300 kgp) reheat Rolls-Royce RB168 Spey 202 turbofans.
Performance: Approx max speed, 1,188 mph (1 912 km/h) above 36,090 ft (11 000 m), or Mach = 1·8. No further details available.
Weights: No details available at time of closing for press.
Armament: One 23-mm twin-barrel cannon, two close-range self-defence AAMs at wingtips and various combinations of bombs and surface-to-air missiles (including CS 801 anti-shipping missiles) on six underwing stores stations.
Status: First of three prototypes rolled out in August 1988 was scheduled to fly during following November. Delivery of series aircraft scheduled for 1993–94.
Notes: The most ambitious Chinese combat aircraft project so far revealed, the H-7 (or, in westernised form, B-7) is in a similar category to the Sukhoi Su-24 *Fencer*, and is intended to be manufactured in dedicated versions for both the PRCAF (People's Republic of China Air Force) and the shore-based air component of the PRCN (People's Republic of China Navy). The prototypes are powered by pattern engines for the Spey licence manufacturing programme which was not pursued, but it is anticipated that series production aircraft will be powered by an indigenous two-spool turbofan, the WS-6 in the 27,500 lb st (12 457 kgp) category. The terrain-following radar and avionics to be installed are allegedly of Chinese design.

Dimensions: (Estimated) Span, 41 ft 6 in (12,65 m); length (excluding nose probe), 61 ft 0 in (18,60 m).

AÉROSPATIALE AS 332L SUPER PUMA

Country of Origin: France.
Type: Medium transport helicopter.
Power Plant: Two 1,877 sph Turboméca Makila 1A1 turboshafts.
Performance: (At 18,960 lb/8 600 kg) Max speed, 173 mph (278 km/h); max cruise, 165 mph (266 km/h) at sea level; max inclined climb, 1,594 ft/min (8,1 m/sec); hovering ceiling (in ground effect), 10,170 ft (3 100 m), (out of ground effect), 7,545 ft (2 300 m); range (standard tankage), 540 mls (870 km).
Weights: Empty, 9,745 lb (4 420 kg); max take-off, 18,960 lb (8 600 kg), (with external load), 20,615 lb (9 350 kg).
Dimensions: Rotor diam, 51 ft 2½ in (15,60 m); fuselage length (tail rotor included), 53 ft 5½ in (16,29 m).
Notes: The AS 332L is an uprated commercial version of the basic AS 332 which first flew on 13 September 1978. The AS 332L1 and its equivalent military AS 332M1 were introduced in 1986, and are the current Super Puma production models. The AS 332L accommodates a crew of two and up to 24 passengers and the AS 332M can carry 25 troops. By the beginning of 1989, in excess of 300 Super Pumas (all versions) had been ordered with more than 250 delivered, the most recent orders having been placed by Brazil, Nigeria and Venezuela. A navalised version, the AS 332F1, has an overall length (including tail rotor) of 50 ft 11½ in (15,53 m), folding rotor blades and folding tail rotor pylon, and is suitable for ASW, anti-ship and search and rescue roles. Customers include the Chilean Navy.

AÉROSPATIALE AS 350B ECUREUIL

Country of Origin: France.
Type: Five/six-seat light utility helocopter.
Power Plant: One 684 shp Turboméca Arriel 1D turboshaft.
Performance: (At 4,850 lb/2 200 kg) Max speed, 178 mph (287 km/h); max cruise, 144 mph (232 km/h); max inclined climb, 1,732 ft/min (8,8 m/sec); hovering ceiling (in ground effect), 9,400 ft (2 870 m), (out of ground effect), 6,560 ft (2 000 m); range (max fuel), 407 mls (655 km).
Weights: Empty, 2,469 lb (1 120 kg); max take-off, 4,850 lb (2 200 kg), (with external load), 5,400 lb (2 450 kg).
Dimensions: Rotor diam, 35 ft 0¾ in (10,69 m); fuselage length (tail rotor included), 35 ft 10½ in (10,93 m).
Notes: The AS 350B1 is the current basic production model of the single-engined Ecureuil (Squirrel), its military equivalent being the AS 350L1, and a version for the North American market is the AS 350D AStar Mk III (with a Textron Lycoming LTS 101-600A-3 turboshaft). The first prototype AS 350 was flown on 27 June 1974, and in excess of 1,200 had been ordered by the beginning of 1989, the AStar being assembled at Grand Prairie, Texas. The AS 350 is also licence-manufactured in Brazil by Helibras as the HB 350 Esquilo. An armed version of the AS 350L1 with a Saab/Emerson Electric HeliTOW anti-armour missile system has been supplied to the Danish Army (12). An AS 350 fitted with a 'fenestron' shrouded tail rotor has been tested, but this is not expected to become a feature of currently envisaged production series.

AÉROSPATIALE AS 355F2 ECUREUIL 2

Country of Origin: France.

Type: Six-seat light general-purpose utility helicopter.

Power Plant: Two 420 shp Allison 250-C20F turboshafts.

Performance: (At 5,600 lb/2 540 kg) Max speed, 169 mph (272 km/h); max cruise, 139 mph (224 km/h) at sea level; max inclined climb, 1,338 ft/min (6,8 m/sec); hovering ceiling (in ground effect), 6,560 ft (2 000 m), (out of ground effect), 4,920 ft (1 500 m); range (max fuel), 437 mls (703 km).

Weights: Empty, 2,877 lb (1 305 kg); max take-off, 5,600 lb (2 540 kg), (with external load), 5,732 lb (2 600 kg).

Dimensions: Rotor diam, 35 ft 0¾ in (10,69 m); fuselage length (tail rotor included), 35 ft 10⅓ in (10,93 m).

Notes: First flown on 27 September 1979, the Ecureuil 2 employs an essentially similar airframe and similar dynamic components to those of the single-engined AS 350 (see page 219). From 1986, the production models have been the AS 355F2 (civil) and AS 355M2 (military) offering increased maximum take-off weights by comparison with preceding production models. The AS 355M2 can be armed with a 20-mm cannon, machine guns or rocket launchers for the fire support mission, and a shipboard version with Bendix 1500 search radar and provision for two torpedoes was under test at the beginning of 1989. At this time, some 400 Ecureuil 2s has been ordered, a version known as the TwinStar was being assembled at Grand Prairie, Texas, and licence production was being undertaken in Brazil by Helibras as the HB 355 Esquilo for both civil and military use.

AÉROSPATIALE SA 365N DAUPHIN 2

Country of Origin: France.
Type: Light multi-purpose and transport helicopter.
Power Plant: Two 724 shp Turboméca Arriel 1C1 turboshafts.
Performance: Max speed, 184 mph (296 km/h); max cruise, 176 mph (283 km/h) at sea level; econ cruise, 161 mph (260 km/h); max inclined climb, 1,300 ft/min (6,6 m/sec); hovering ceiling (in ground effect), 6,890 ft (2 100 m), (out of ground effect), 3,610 ft (1 100 m); range (standard fuel), 530 mls (852 km).
Weights: Empty, 4,764 lb (2 161 kg); max take-off, 9,039 lb (4 100 kg).
Dimensions: Rotor diam, 39 ft 2 in (11,94 m); fuselage length (tail rotor included), 38 ft 1⅞ in (11,63 m).
Notes: The SA 365 Dauphin 2 was flown as a prototype on 31 March 1979, and is currently offered in four versions, the 8–13 passenger SA 365N (described and illustrated above), the military SA 365M Panther (see 1988 edition) with provision for roof-mounted sight and various weapon options, the navalised SA 365F with folding rotor, Agrion radar and four AS 15TT anti-ship missiles (of which 20 acquired by Saudi Arabia) and the SA 366G, a Textron Lycoming LTS 101-750-powered search and rescue version for the US Coast Guard. Ninety of the last-mentioned variant have been procured by the US Coast Guard as HH-65A Dolphins. Some 400 (all versions) had been purchased by the beginning of 1989, including 50 built in China as the HAMC Z-9 Haitun (Dolphin).

AGUSTA A 109A MK II

Country of Origin: Italy.

Type: Eight-seat light utility helicopter.

Power Plant: Two 420 shp Allison 250-C20B turboshafts.

Performance: (At 5,402 lb/2 450 kg) Max speed, 193 mph (311 km/h); max cruise, 172 mph (278 km/h); econ cruise, 145 mph (233 km/h); max inclined climb, 1,820 ft/min (9,25 m/sec); hovering ceiling (in ground effect), 7,900 ft (2 410 m), (out of ground effect), 6,800 ft (2 073 m); range (standard fuel), 392 mls (631 km).

Weights: Empty equipped, 3,125 lb (1 418 kg); max take-off, 5,732 lb (2 600 kg).

Dimensions: Rotor diam, 36 ft 1 in (11,00 m); fuselage length, 35 ft 1½ in (10,71 m).

Notes: The A 109A Mk II, which supplanted the initial series model in 1981, is being offered in a variety of specialised civil, military, naval and police versions, the latest of these being the A 109EOA FEBA (Forward Edge of the Battle Area) scout, delivery of 24 of which to the Italian Army commenced mid 1988. The A 109EOA features an elongated nose, a fixed undercarriage, an Allison 250-C20R/1 with a new transmission and an increased loaded weight. Agusta had delivered some 200 A 109A Mk IIs (all versions) by the beginning of 1989, these following approximately 150 earlier models. Aerial scout, light attack, command and control, medevac and utility versions have been supplied to a number of armed forces, including those of Argentina, Libya and Yugoslavia.

AGUSTA A 129 MANGUSTA

Country of Origin: Italy.
Type: Two-seat light anti-armour, attack and scout helicopter.
Power Plant: Two 915 shp Rolls-Royce Gem 2 Mk 1004D turboshafts.
Performance: (At 8,157 lb/3 700 kg) Max speed, 161 mph (259 km/h) at sea level; short endurance dash, 196 mph (315 km/h); max inclined climb, 2,150 ft/min (10,92 m/sec); hovering ceiling (in ground effect), 12,300 ft (3 750 m), (out of ground effect), 9,900 ft (3 015 m); max endurance, 3·0 hrs.
Weights: Empty equipped, 5,575 lb (2 529 kg); max take-off, 9,039 lb (4 100 kg).
Dimensions: Rotor diam, 39 ft 0½ in (11,90 m); fuselage length, 40 ft 3¼ in (12,27 m).
Notes: Developed to meet an Italian Army requirement, the A 129 Mangusta (Mongoose) first flew (first of five flying prototypes) on 11 September 1983, and approval has been given for an initial production batch of 60 helicopters of this type to equip two Italian Army Aviation squadrons with deliveries commencing mid 1989. A requirement exists for a further 30 A 129s to equip a third squadron, and a production rate of three monthly is to be attained during 1989. The A 129 has four underwing stores stations, all stressed for loads up to 661 lb (300 kg), and basic armament comprises eight TOW anti-armour missiles with a Saab/Emerson HeliTOW launch system. With these can be carried 7,62-mm, 12,7-mm or 20-mm gun pods, or 14 air-to-surface rockets on two launchers.

BELL AH-1F COBRA/TOW

Country of Origin: USA.
Type: Two-seat light anti-armour and attack helicopter.
Power Plant: One 1,800 shp Textron Lycoming T53-L-703
turboshaft.
Performance: (TOW configuration) Max speed, 141 mph
(227 km/h); max inclined climb, 1,620 ft/min (8,23 m/sec);
hovering ceiling (in ground effect), 12,200 ft (3 720 m); range
(max fuel and 8 per cent reserves), 315 mls (507 km) at sea
level.
Weights: Operational empty, 6,598 lb (2 993 kg); max take-
off, 10,000 lb (4 535 kg).
Dimensions: Rotor diam, 44 ft 0 in (13,41 m); fuselage length,
44 ft 7 in (13,59 m).
Notes: A total of 378 AH-1G and -1Q Cobras were retrofitted
with the TOW missile system and a T53-L-703 engine as AH-1S
Cobra/TOW helicopters. The first 100 new-build AH-1S helicopters have since been redesignated as AH-1Ps, the next 98
(with enhanced armament system) becoming as AH-1Es, and the
final production version, originally known as the 'Modernised
AH-1S' (new fire control system with a a laser rangefinder and
tracker, ballistics computer, head-up display, Doppler navigation system and new composite rotor blades) is designated AH-
1F. Ninety-nine were built for the US Army and 50 for the Air
National Guard. The AH-1S is being assembled in Japan by Fuji
Heavy Industries for the Ground Self-Defence Force which has
a requirement for 73.

BELL AH-1W SUPERCOBRA

Country of Origin: USA.
Type: Two-seat light anti-armour and attack helicopter.
Power Plant: Two 1,690 shp General Electric T700-GE-401 turboshafts.
Performance: (At 14,750 lb/6 690 kg) Max speed, 175 mph (282 km/h) at sea level; max cruise, 173 mph (278 km/h); hovering ceiling (in ground effect), 14,750 ft (4 495 m), (out of ground effect), 3,000 ft (914 m); range (standard fuel), 395 mls (635 km) at sea level.
Weights: Empty, 10,200 lb (4 627 kg); max take-off, 14,750 lb (6 690 kg).
Dimensions: Rotor diam, 48 ft 0 in (14,63 m); fuselage length, 45 ft 6 in (13,87 m).
Notes: The AH-1W SuperCobra was first flown on 16 November 1983 as an enhanced-capability derivative of the AH-1T SeaCobra of the US Marine Corps. This service now has 44 AH-1Ws in its inventory, will receive 30 between June 1990 and June 1991, and is planning conversion of 39 AH-1Ts to AH-1W standard. The primary Marine Corps mission of the AH-1W is the escort of troop-carrying helicopters for which it carries two AIM-9L AAMs in addition to the triple-barrel 20-mm cannon in the nose barbette. For the anti-armour role it can carry up to eight TOW or Hellfire launch-and-leave missiles, and for landing zone suppression and close-in fire support, 76 folding-fin 2·75-in rockets, 16 Zuni 5-in rockets or two GPU-2A 20-mm self-contained cannon pods may be carried.

BELL MODEL 214ST SUPERTRANSPORT

Country of Origin: USA.

Type: Medium transport helicopter (18 passengers).

Power Plant: Two 1,625 shp General Electric CT7-2A turbo-shafts.

Performance: Max cruise, 159 mph (256 km/h) at 4,000 ft (1 220 m), 161 mph (259 km/h) at sea level; max inclined climb rate, 1,780 ft/min (9,04 m/sec); hovering ceiling (in ground effect), 6,400 ft (1 950 m); range (max standard fuel), 533 mls (858 km) at 4,000 ft (1 220 m); ferry range (with auxiliary fuel), 633 mls (1 019 km).

Weights: Max take-off (internal or external load), 17,500 lb (7 938 kg).

Dimensions: Rotor diam, 52 ft 0 in (15,85 m); fuselage length, 49 ft 3¾ in (15,02 m).

Notes: A significantly improved derivative of the Model 214B BigLifter, the Model 214ST SuperTransport flew for the first time in February 1977, customer deliveries commencing early in 1982. By the beginning of 1989, some 90 SuperTransport helicopters had been delivered to civil and military customers, the latter including Brunei (1), Iraq (20), Peru (11), Thailand (9) and Venezuela (4). In commercial use a crew of two and 18 passengers may be carried in airline seating, a non-retractable tubular skid-type or tricycle wheel-type undercarriages may be fitted, and a variety of special mission equipment has been developed and certified to suit the Model 214ST for service with the offshore oil industry. A 7,000-lb (3 175-kg) slung load may be carried.

BELL MODEL 222UT

Country of Origin: USA.
Type: Six/eight-seat light utility and transport helicopter.
Power Plant: Two 684 shp Textron Lycoming LTS 101-750C-1 turboshafts.
Performance: Max speed, 172 mph (278 km/h) at sea level, 179 mph (289 km/h) at 4,000 ft (1 220 m); econ cruise, 153 mph (246 km/h) at 4,000 ft (1 220 m); max inclined climb, 1,680 ft/min (8,53 m/sec); hovering ceiling (in ground effect), 7,100 ft (2 165 m), (out of ground effect), 6,400 ft (1 950 m); range (max fuel), 429 mls (691 km).
Weights: Empty equipped, 4,874 lb (2 210 kg); max take-off, 8,250 lb (3 742 kg).
Dimensions: Rotor diam, 42 ft 0 in (12,80 m); fuselage length, 42 ft 2 in (12,85 m).
Notes: The Model 222UT (Utility Twin) is similar to the basic Model 222B apart from having a tubular skid rather than retractable wheel undercarriage. The first of five prototypes of the Model 222 flew for the first time on 13 August 1976, with initial customer deliveries commencing on 16 January 1980. The Models 222B and 222UT have larger main rotor and uprated power plant by comparison with the initial production version, and some 180 (all versions) had been delivered by the beginning of 1989. The Model 222B was the first transport category helicopter to be certificated by the FAA for single-pilot IFR flight without stability augmentation. An executive version for five-six passengers is available.

BELL MODEL 406CS

Country of Origin: USA.

Type: Light multi-purpose military helicopter.

Power Plant: One 650 shp Allison 250-C30L turboshaft.

Performance: (At 4,500 lb/2 041 kg) Max speed, 150 mph (240 km/h); max cruise, 138 mph (222 km/h); hovering ceiling (in ground effect), 19,800 ft (6 035 m), (out of ground effect), 17,100 ft (5 210 m); range (max fuel), 250 mls (402 km); endurance, 2·6 hrs.

Weights: Empty, 2,266 lb (1 028 kg); max take-off, 4,500 lb (2 041 kg).

Dimensions: Rotor diam, 35 ft 0 in (10,67 m); fuselage length, 33 ft 10 in (10,31 m).

Notes: First flown in June 1984, the Model 406CS (Combat Scout) is a lighter and simplified variant of the US Army's AHIP (Army Helicopter Improvement Program) OH-58D equipped with a quick-change weapons system. Embodying many AHIP features, the Combat Scout can carry an armament of two GIAT 20-mm gun pods, four TOW 2 anti-armour missiles, or a mix of Stinger AAMs, 70-mm rockets and 7,62-mm or 0·5-in guns. Fifteen Combat Scouts are being procured for the Saudi Arabian Army. Fifteen AHIP OH-58Ds have been equipped with armament as AH-58D Warriors and additional helicopters are to be similarly converted. The US Army plans to convert at least 578 existing OH-58A Kiowa helicopters to AHIP OH-58D standards, and of these a total of 207 had been funded by the beginning of 1989. The AHIP configuration includes a mast-mounted sight.

BELL MODEL 412SP

Country of Origin: Canada (USA).
Type: Fifteen-seat utility transport helicopter.
Power Plant: One 1,400 shp Pratt & Whitney Canada PT6T-3B Turbo Twin Pac twin turboshaft.
Performance: (At 11,900 lb/5 397 kg) Max speed, 161 mph (259 km/h) at sea level; max cruise, 143 mph (230 km/h); max inclined climb, 1,350 ft/min (6,86 m/sec); hovering ceiling (in ground effect), 1,400 ft (427 m); max range (standard fuel), 408 mls (656 km) at sea level.
Weights: Empty, 6,495 lb (2 946 kg); max take-off, 11,900 lb (5 397 kg).
Dimensions: Rotor diam, 46 ft 0 in (14,02 m); fuselage length, 42 ft 4¾ in (12,92 m).
Notes: The Model 412SP (Special Performance) is the latest version of the Model 412 which was first flown in August 1979, with customer deliveries commencing on 18 January 1981. The Model 412SP has an increased max take-off weight and uprated transmission, and licence manufacture is undertaken in Indonesia by IPTN which is producing 100 helicopters of this type. All production of the Model 412 was transferred from the USA to Mirabel, Quebec, Canada, at the beginning of 1989. A military version of the Model 412SP has been developed, and during 1988 armament qualification trials were being conducted, and Agusta, the Italian licensee, has evolved its own multi-role military version known as the Griffon. This can perform medevac, armed tactical support, SAR and patrol missions.

BOEING HELICOPTERS MODEL 414-100

Country of Origin: USA.
Type: Medium transport helicopter.
Power Plant: Two 4,378 shp Textron Lycoming T55-L-712 SSB turboshafts.
Performance: (At 50,000 lb/22 680 kg) Max speed, 171 mph (276 km/h) at sea level; service ceiling, 9,100 ft (2 775 m); hovering ceiling (out of ground effect), 6,100 ft (1 860 m), radius (with 15,733-lb/7 136-kg internal payload and 20 min reserves), 115 mls (185 km) at 4,000 ft (1 220 m).
Weights: Max take-off, 54,000 lb (24 494 kg).
Dimensions: Rotor diam (each), 60 ft 0 in (18,29 m); fuselage length, 51 ft 0 in (15,55 m).
Notes: The Model 414-100, or CH-47D International Chinook, first flew in January 1986 as an upgraded export Model 414, the international military version of the CH-47C (illustrated above). The commercial equivalent is the Model 234 (4,075 shp Textron Lycoming AL 5512 engines), which is offered in long-range (234LR), extended-range (234ER), utility (234UT) and multi-purpose long-range (234MLR) versions. Earlier US Army versions of the Chinook (CH-47A, -47B, and -47C) are being rotated through a remanufacturing programme as CH-47Ds, this embracing a total of 472 helicopters and 265 had been restored to US Army service by the beginning of 1989, when the conversion rate was four monthly. The CH-47D has a useful load capability of 22,783 lb (10 334 kg). The Model 414-100 is being licence-built in Japan (as the CH-47J) for both the Ground and Air Self-Defence Forces.

EH INDUSTRIES EH 101

Country of Origin: United Kingdom and Italy.
Type: Military and commercial transport, utility and shipboard anti-submarine warfare helicopter.
Power Plant: Three (civil and military transports) 1,920 shp General Electric CT7-6 or (naval variant) 1,714 shp T700-GE-401A turboshafts.
Performance: (Manufacturer's estimates at 31,500 lb/14 288 kg) Average cruise speed, 184 mph (296 km/h); range cruise, 161 mph (259 km/h); hovering ceiling (in ground effect), 9,000 ft (2 745 m), (out of ground effect), 5,500 ft (1 675 m;) range (standard fuel and 30 passengers), 576 mls (926 km); ferry range (with auxiliary fuel), 921 mls (1 482 km).
Weights: (Estimated) Empty (naval version), 15,700 lb (7 121 kg), (commercial), 15,360 lb (6 967 kg); max take-off (naval version), 28,660 lb (13 000 kg), (commercial), 31,500 lb (14 288 kg).
Dimensions: Rotor diam, 61 ft 0 in (18,59 m); overall length (rotors turning), 74 ft 10 in (22,81 m).
Notes: EH Industries (comprising Westland Helicopters of the UK and Agusta of Italy) has been formed specifically for the development of the EH 101 multi-role helicopter, the first of nine pre-series aircraft having flown on 9 October 1987. The naval EH 101 is designed for both shipboard and land-based operations, is expected to be delivered to the British and Italian Navies from 1990, and has been selected by Canada for its naval aviation component. The 30-passenger commercial version will be certificated in 1991.

KAMOV KA-27 (HELIX)

Country of Origin: USSR.

Type: Shipboard anti-submarine warfare, assault transport and search-and-rescue helicopter.

Power Plant: Two 2,225 shp Isotov TV-117V turboshafts.

Performance: Max speed, 155 mph (250 km/h); max continuous cruise, 143 mph (230 km/h); max range, 497 mls (800 km); service ceiling (at 24,250 lb/11 000 kg), 16,405 ft (5 000 m).

Weights: Normal loaded, 24,250 lb (11 000 kg); max loaded (with external slung load), 27,778 lb (12 600 kg).

Dimensions: Rotor diam (each), 52 ft 1$\frac{7}{8}$ in (15,90 m); overall length, 37 ft 0$\frac{7}{8}$ in (11,30 m).

Notes: The Ka-27, first observed in ASW form (Helix-A) in the Baltic in September 1981, has been developed for both military and civil roles. An air assault version (Helix-B) is operated from amphibious warships and a search and rescue version (Helix-D), illustrated above, has a hoist above the port cabin door and rectangular pods on the fuselage sides. An export ASW version, the Ka-28, has been supplied to Yugoslavia, and several civil versions (Helix-C) have been developed as the Ka-32. These are offered as passenger or freight helicopters, accommodating up to 16 people or 8,818 lb (4 000 kg) or cargo internally, or an externally slung load of 11,023 lb (5 000 kg). An adverse-weather, day or night dedicated ASR version equivalent to Helix-D is designated Ka-32S. The Helix also serves aboard the atomic-powered icebreakers *Lenin*, *Sibir*, *Arktika* and *Rossiya*.

KAMOV KA-126 (HOODLUM-B)

Country of Origin: USSR (Romania).
Type: Light utility helicopter.
Power Plant: One 720 shp Kopchenko TVD-100 turboshaft.
Performance: Max speed, 112 mph (180 km/h); max continuous cruise, 99 mph (160 km/h); hovering ceiling (in ground effect), 3,280 ft (1 000 m); service ceiling, 12,630 ft (3 850 m); max range, 404 mls (650 km).
Weights: Max take-off, 7,165 lb (3 250 kg).
Dimensions: Rotor diam, 42 ft 7¾ in (13,00 m); fuselage length, 25 ft 5⅛ in (7,75 m).
Notes: Flown for the first time in May 1988, development having been delayed some two years owing to protracted testing of the intended turboshaft, the Ka-126 is fundamentally an upgraded and re-engined Ka-26 (Hoodlum) twin piston-engined helicopter, some 850 of which were built, including 300 for export. The majority of the surviving Ka-26s are expected to be rotated through a conversion programme to Ka-126 standards which is to be undertaken in Romania by ICA Brasov, the first Romanian Ka-126 being scheduled to enter flight test during 1989. Like the Ka-26, the Ka-126 comprises a small, extensively-glazed crew cabin forward of the rotor mast and two tail booms, the space aft of the cabin beneath the rotor mast and engine being able to accommodate a variety of interchangeable payloads, these including a pod capable of accommodating four/six passengers or an equivalent freight load. Installation of a turboshaft results in a significant increase in payload.

MBB BO 105LS A-3

Country of Origin: Canada (Federal Germany).
Type: Five/six-seat light utility helicopter.
Power Plant: Two 550 shp Allison 250-C28C turboshafts.
Performance: (At 5,732 lb/2 600 kg) Max speed, 155 mph
(250 km/h) at sea level; max cruise, 148 mph (239 km/h) at sea
level; max inclined climb, 1,790 ft/min (9,1 m/sec); hovering
ceiling (in ground effect) 11,500 ft (3 505 m), (out of ground
effect), 7,380 ft (2 250 m); range (standard fuel), 320 mls
(515 km); ferry range (with two 44 Imp gal/200 l auxiliary tanks),
547 mls (880 km).
Weights: Basic empty, 3,047 lb (1 182 kg); max take-off,
5,732 lb (2 600 kg).
Dimensions: Rotor diam, 32 ft 3½ in (9,84 m); fuselage length,
28 ft 11 in (8,81 m).
Notes: The BO 105LS (Lift and Stretch) is being manufactured
by MBB Helicopter Canada Ltd at Fort Erie, and combines the
enlarged cabin of the CBS version (illustrated above) with
more powerful engines and an uprated transmission system.
The BO 105LS first flew on 23 October 1981, technology and
design authority subsequently being transferred to the Canadian
subsidiary with the LS A-3 model, the first customer delivery
being made in February 1987. At the beginning of 1989, testing
was proceeding of a further development, the LS B-1 with Pratt
& Whitney Canada PW205B turboshafts, and some 1,270 BO
105 helicopters (all models) had been delivered. Licence
manufacture was continuing in Indonesia by IPTN.

MBB BO 108

Country of Origin: Federal Germany.
Type: Four/five-seat light utility helicopter.
Power Plant: Two 450 shp Allison 250-C20R3 turboshafts.
Performance: Max speed, 168 mph (270 km/h) at 4,920 ft (1 500 m); optimum cruise, 149 mph (240 km/h); max climb, 1,810 ft/min (9,2 m/sec); hovering ceiling (in ground effect), 12,630 ft (3 850 m), (out of ground effect), 10,990 ft (3 350 m); normal range, 516 mls (830 km).
Weights: Empty, 2,700 lb (1 225 kg); max take-off, 5,291 lb (2 400 kg).
Dimensions: Rotor diam, 32 ft $9\frac{7}{10}$ in (10,00 m); fuselage length, 31 ft 3 in (9,52 m).
Notes: Essentially a technology demonstrator to assess the potential of advanced systems and sub-systems integrated into a new airframe, the BO 108 was first flown on 15 October 1988, and a second prototype is scheduled to join the test programme in the autumn of 1989. Designed to offer significant improvements in performance and operating costs, the BO 108 has a bearingless four-blade main rotor of composite construction, a hingeless elastomeric two-blade composite tail rotor, a simplified transmission system and a largely composite airframe. Development of the BO 108 has been funded by MBB and various equipment manufacturers, the aim being to combine in one helicopter the latest technological developments. No plans for series production of the BO 108 had been announced by the beginning of 1989.

MBB-KAWASAKI BK 117 B-1

Countries of Origin: Federal Germany and Japan.
Type: Multi-purpose eight/twelve-seat helicopter.
Power Plant: Two 592 shp Textron Lycoming LTS 101-750B-1 turboshafts.
Performance: (At 7,055 lb/3 200 kg) Max speed, 172 mph (278 km/h) at sea level; max cruise, 154 mph (248 km/h); max inclined climb, 1,910 ft/min (9,7 m/sec); hovering ceiling (in ground effect), 9,600 ft (2 925 m), (out of ground effect), 7,500 ft (2 285 m); range (max standard fuel), 354 mls (570 km); ferry range (with 44 Imp gal/200 l of auxiliary fuel), 460 mls (740 km).
Weights: Basic empty, 3,807 lb (1 727 kg); max take-off, 7,055 lb (3 200 kg).
Dimensions: Rotor diam, 36 ft 1 in (11,00 m); fuselage length, 32 ft 6¼ in (9,91 m).
Notes: The BK 117 B-1 was the standard production version of the BK 117 at the beginning of 1989. Developed jointly by MBB of Germany and Kawasaki of Japan, the BK 117 is manufactured by the single-source method, each company producing the components that it has developed which are then exchanged. German and Japanese components are also supplied to assembly lines in Canada (MBB Helicopters Canada) and Indonesia (IPTN), the latter producing the aircraft under licence as the NBK 117. Customer deliveries of the initial BK 117 A-1 model began early in 1981, the progressively improved A-3 and A-4 giving place to the B-1 certificated in 1987.

McDONNELL DOUGLAS 500E

Country of Origin: USA.
Type: Light commercial utility helicopter.
Power Plant: One 375 shp Allison 250-C20B turboshaft.
Performance: Max cruise speed, 160 mph (258 km/h) at sea level, 154 mph (248 km/h) at 5,000 ft (1 525 m); econ cruise, 148 mph (238 km/h) at sea level; max inclined climb, 1,875 ft/min (9,52 m/sec); hovering ceiling (in ground effect), 8,500 ft (2 590 m), (out of ground effect), 6,100 ft (1 860 m); range, 320 mls (515 km/h) at 5,000 ft (1 525 m).
Weights: Empty, 1,441 lb (654 kg); max take-off (normal), 3,000 lb (1 361 kg), (overload), 3550 lb (1 610 kg).
Dimensions: Rotor diam, 26 ft 4 in (8,03 m); fuselage length, 23 ft 11 in (7,29 m).
Notes: The Model 500 first entered production in November 1968 as a civil development of the OH-6A Cayuse military scout, and more than 4,000 helicopters of the Model 500 (and 530) series had been built by the beginning of 1989. The Model 500E, introduced in 1982, differed from its predecessor, the Model 500D, primarily in having a lengthened, more streamlined fuselage nose, a new auxiliary fuel tank and a four-blade tail rotor. More than 300 had been delivered by the end of 1988, and licence manufacture was being undertaken by BredaNardi in Italy, up to 50 being required by the Italian Air Force for training duties. Certification of a version with an Allison 250-C20R, the Model 520L, was anticipated late 1988. The Model 520N is an experimental version without tail rotor.

McDONNELL DOUGLAS 530MG/TOW DEFENDER

Country of Origin: USA.
Type: Light gunship and anti-armour helicopter.
Power Plant: One 425 shp Allison 250-C30 turboshaft.
Performance: Max speed, 150 mph (241 km/h) at sea level; max cruise, 137 mph (221 km/h) at sea level, 140 mph (226 km/h) at 5,000 ft (1 525 m); max inclined climb, 2,070 ft/min (10,51 m/sec); hovering ceiling (in ground effect), 16,600 ft (5 060 m), (out of ground effect), 14,100 ft (4 300 m); range (standard fuel), 233 mls (376 km) at 5,000 ft (1 525 m).
Weights: Normal loaded, 3,100 lb (1 406 kg); max take-off, 3,550 lb (1 610 kg).
Dimensions: Rotor diam, 27 ft 4 in (8,33 m); fuselage length, 23 ft 11 in (7,29 m).
Notes: The Models 530MG and 530MG/TOW (illustrated above) are intended primarily for point attack and anti-armour missions, and are based on the airframe and power plant of the commercial Model 530F Lifter (see 1988 edition) which provides accommodation for pilot and two passengers on a forward bench-type seat, with two or four passengers in the rear portion of the cabin. The Model 530MG can be used for scout, day and night surveillance, utility and light attack tasks, the Model 530MG/TOW differing in having a mast-mounted sighting system and provision for four TOW (tube-launched optically-tracked wire-guided) anti-armour missiles. A version in limited service with the US Army is designated MH-6A, and the Model 530K has increased high altitude capability.

McDONNELL DOUGLAS AH-64A APACHE

Country of Origin: USA.

Type: Tandem two-seat attack helicopter.

Power Plant: Two 1,696 shp General Electric T700-GE-701 turboshafts.

Performance: Max speed (at 14,445 lb/6 552 kg), 225 mph (362 km/h); cruise (anti-armour mission with four Hellfire missiles), 177 mph (285 km/h) at 4,000 ft (1 220 m), (with eight Hellfire missiles), 170 mph (274 km/h) at 2,000 ft (610 m); hovering ceiling (in ground effect), 15,000 ft (4 570 m), (out of ground effect), 11,500 ft (3 505 m); range (internal fuel), 300 mls (482 km).

Weights: Empty, 10,760 lb (4 881 kg); max take-off, 21,000 lb (9 525 kg).

Dimensions: Rotor diam, 48 ft 0 in (14,63 m); fuselage length, 48 ft 1$\frac{7}{8}$ in (14,70 m).

Notes: Flown for the first time on 30 September 1975, the AH-64A was first delivered to the US Army during the summer of 1984, 427 having been delivered by the beginning of 1989 against orders for 665. The US Army has a requirement for a total of 975 AH-64As by the end of the 1994 Fiscal Year. The AH-64A is armed with a single-barrel 30-mm gun based on the chain-driven bolt system and suspended beneath the fuselage, and may carry up to 16 laser-guided Hellfire anti-tank missiles or up to 76 70-mm rockets. To enhance air-to-air and self-defence capability, Stinger, Sidewinder and Mistral AAMs have been integrated with the AH-64A's weapons system.

MIL MI-14 (HAZE)

Country of Origin: USSR.
Type: Amphibious (Haze-A) anti-submarine, (Haze-B) mine countermeasures and (Haze-C) search and rescue helicopter.
Power Plant: Two 1,950 shp Isotov TV-3-117M turboshafts.
Performance: (Haze-A) Max speed, 143 mph (230 km/h) at sea level; max continuous cruise, 124 mph (200 km/h); ceiling, 11,485 ft (3 500 m); range, 705 mls (1 135 km); endurance, 5·93 hrs.
Weights: Max take-off, 30,864 lb (14 000 kg).
Dimensions: Rotor diam, 69 ft 10¼ in (21,29 m); length (rotors turning), 83 ft 0 in (25,30 m).
Notes: Evolved from the Mi-8 transport helicopter, the Mi-14 serves in three basic versions: the Mi-14PL (Haze-A) anti-submarine aircraft with four crew members, Oka-2 sonar equipment and APM-60 magnetometer, and accommodating torpedoes and depth charges in the hull; the Mi-14BT (Haze-B) mine countermeasures aircraft, and the Mi-14PS (Haze-C) search-and-rescue aircraft which carries 10 20-person inflatable rafts, a three-person rescue net and an internally-stowed winch. The Mi-14PL (illustrated above) serves with Bulgaria, Cuba, East Germany, Libya, North Korea, Poland, Romania and Yugoslavia, as well as with the Soviet Navy, and the Mi-14BT also serves with several countries, including East Germany and Poland. The Mi-14 first entered service in 1975, the series version having the same power plant, rotors and transmission systems as the Mi-17 derivative of the Mi-8 transport helicopter.

MIL MI-17 (HIP)

Country of Origin: USSR.

Type: General-purpose transport helicopter.

Power Plant: Two 1,900 shp Isotov TV3-M117MT turboshafts.

Performance: (At 28,660 lb/13 000 kg) Max speed, 155 mph (250 km/h); max continuous cruise, 149 mph (240 km/h); hovering ceiling (out of ground effect at 24,270 lb/11 100 kg), 5,775 ft (1 760 m); service ceiling, 11,800 ft (3 600 m); range (with max standard fuel), 289 mls (465 km), (with auxiliary fuel), 590 mls (950 km).

Weights: Empty equipped, 15,653 lb (7 100 kg); max take-off, 28,660 lb (13 000 kg).

Dimensions: Rotor diam, 69 ft $10\frac{1}{4}$ in (21,29 m); fuselage length, 60 ft $5\frac{3}{8}$ in (18,42 m).

Notes: The Mi-17 is fundamentally a combination of the Mi-8 airframe with uprated Isotov turboshafts, and because of the external similarity, continues the series of suffix letters applied to the reporting name of Hip assigned in the West to the earlier helicopter. The Mi-17 (Hip-H) serves side-by-side with the earlier Mi-8 in the Soviet armed forces, and, like its predecessor, has been widely exported, recipients including Angola, Cuba, India, Nicaragua, North Korea and Peru. The Mi-17 has the same armament options as the Mi-8 (Hip-C, -E and -F), supplemented with 23-mm cannon packs, and including up to 192 rockets in six suspended packs, four Swatter or six Sagger anti-armour missiles and a nose-mounted 12,7-mm gun. In civil form accommodation is provided for a crew of three and 24–28 passengers.

MIL MI-24 (HIND)

Country of Origin: USSR.
Type: Assault and anti-armour helicopter.
Power Plant: Two 2,200 shp Isotov TV3-117 turboshafts.
Performance: (Hind-D) Max speed, 192 mph (310 km/h) at 3,280 ft/1 000 m); max continuous cruise, 183 mph (295 km/h); max inclined climb, 2,460 ft/min (12,5 m/sec); hovering ceiling (out of ground effect), 7,200 ft (2 200 m); service ceiling, 14,750 ft (4 500 m); range (max internal fuel), 466 mls (750 km); combat radius (max ordnance on internal fuel), 99 mls (160 km).
Weights: (Estimated) Empty, 18,520 lb (8 400 kg); normal loaded, 24,250 lb (11 000 kg).
Dimensions: (Estimated) Rotor diam, 55 ft 0 in (16,76 m); fuselage length (excluding gun), 57 ft 6 in (17,52 m).
Notes: Derived from the Hind-A armed assault helicopter, the optimised gunship versions of the Mi-24 feature a redesigned forward fuselage with vertically-staggered tandem stations for the weapons operator and pilot, but retain accommodation for an eight-man assault squad. The basic version (Hind-D) has a barbette-mounted 12,7-mm four-barrel rotary gun in a nose barbette and carries up to 3,300 lb (1 500 kg) of external ordnance. This has been widely exported as the Mi-25 (illustrated above). The Hind-E has provision for 12 AT-6 (Spiral) anti-tank missiles; the Hind-F has the gun barbette replaced by a fixed twin-barrel 30-mm cannon, and Hind-G is a special-mission version. The Mi-35 is an upgraded version with additional armour and new avionics.

MIL MI-26 (HALO)

Country of Origin: USSR.

Type: Military and commercial heavy-lift helicopter.

Power Plant: Two 11,240 shp Lotarev D-136 turboshafts.

Performance: Max speed, 183 mph (295 km/h); normal cruise, 158 mph (255 km/h); hovering ceiling (in ground effect), 14,765 ft (4 500 m), (out of ground effect), 5,905 ft (1 800 m); range (at 109,127 lb/49 500 kg), 310 mls (500 km), (at 123,457 lb/ 56 000 kg), 497 mls (800 km).

Weights: Empty, 62,169 lb (28 200 kg); normal loaded, 109,227 lb (49 500 kg); max take-off, 123,457 lb (56 000 kg).

Dimensions: Rotor diam, 104 ft $11\frac{7}{8}$ in (32,00 m); fuselage length (nose to tail rotor), 110 ft $7\frac{3}{4}$ in (33,73 m).

Notes: The Mi-26 is the heaviest and most powerful helicopter yet flown, entering flight test on 14 December 1977, with pre-series production commencing in 1980, full-scale production beginning in 1981. The Mi-26 features an innovative eight-bladed main rotor, carries a flight crew of five and has a maximum internal payload of 44,090 lb (20 000 kg). The freight hold is larger than that of the fixed-wing An-12 transport and at least 70 combat-equipped troops or 40 casualty stretchers may be accommodated. Although allegedly developed to meet a civil requirement, the primary role of the Mi-26 is obviously military, and the SovAF achieved initial operational capability with the series version late 1983. An initial batch of 10 Mi-26s has been supplied to the Indian Air Force, with a similar batch following in 1989.

MIL MI-28 (HAVOC)

Country of Origin: USSR.

Type: Tandem two-seat anti-armour and attack helicopter.

Power Plant: Two 2,000–2,500 shp turboshafts (possibly related to the Isotov TV3-117).

Performance: (Estimated) Max speed, 186 mph (300 km/h) at sea level; tactical radius, 149 mls (240 km).

Weights: (Estimated) Max take-off, 17,635 lb (8 000 kg).

Dimensions: (Estimated) Rotor diam, 55 ft 9 in (17,00 m); fueslage length (tail rotor included), 57 ft 1 in (17,40 m).

Notes: Unlike the Mi-24 (Hind), the Mi-28 possesses no transport capability, being a dedicated attack helicopter with emphasis on agility and survivability. Development of the Mi-28 is believed to have commenced in the early 'eighties, and it is expected to be deployed by Soviet attack helicopter regiments during 1989-90. Apparently closely comparable in size and performance with the AH-64 Apache, the Mi-28, the above illustration of which should be considered as provisional, has a single large calibre gun (probably a multi-barrel 23-mm weapon) in an undernose barbette, and pylons beneath each stub wing are expected to carry four launching pods each containing four laser-guided anti-armour missiles, plus tube-launched missiles at the wingtips for self-defence or air-ground use. The structure of the Mi-28 is believed to embody integral armour around the area of the tandem cockpits, and noteworthy features include the pod-mounted engines and upwardly-deflected exhaust pipes.

MIL MI-34 (HERMIT)

Country of Origin: USSR.

Type: Two/four-seat light instructional and competition helicopter.

Power Plant: One 325 hp Vedeneyev M-14V-26 nine-cylinder radial air-cooled engine.

Performance: Max speed (at normal loaded weight), 130 mph (210 km/h); max cruise, 112 mph (180 km/h); hovering ceiling (in ground effect), 4,920 ft (1 500 m); service ceiling, 14,765 ft (4 500 m); range (max take-off weight and 364-lb/165-kg payload), 112 mls (180 km), (198-lb/90-kg payload), 280 mls (450 km).

Weights: Normal loaded, 2,249 lb (1 020 kg); max take-off, 2,755 lb (1 250 kg).

Dimensions: Rotor diam, 32 ft 9¾ in (10,00 m); fuselage length, 28 ft 7 in (8,71 m).

Notes: The first of two prototypes of the Mi-34 was flown late in 1986, and series production is expected to commence during the course of 1989. While primarily intended for tuitional and competition purposes, the Mi-34 is suited for light utility, observation and liaison tasks, and manufacture of more than 1,000 helicopters of this type is projected. Consideration is also being given to a derivative with a small turboshaft engine. Normally one or two pilots are accommodated side-by-side, with optional dual controls, but a bench seat for two passengers may be installed as an option to a flat floor for freight. Series production may be undertaken in Poland by WSK-PZL.

ROBINSON R22 MARINER

Country of Origin: USA.

Type: Two-seat light utility helicopter.

Power Plant: One 160 hp Textron Lycoming 0-320-B2C four-cylinder horizontally-opposed piston engine.

Performance: Max speed, 112 mph (180 km/h); cruise speed (75% power), 110 mph (177 km/h) at 8,000 ft (2 440 m); hovering ceiling (in ground effect), 6,970 ft (2 125 m); service ceiling, 14,000 ft (4 265 m); (range (max payload and auxiliary fuel), 368 mls (592 km).

Weights: Empty, 824 lb (374 kg); max take-off, 1,370 lb (621 kg).

Dimensions: Rotor diam, 25 ft 2 in (7,67 m); fuselage length, 20 ft 8 in (6,30 m).

Notes: The R22 was flown in prototype form for the first time on 28 August 1975, production deliveries commencing in October 1979, and it has since been in continuous production in progressively improved versions, with some 940 delivered by the beginning of 1989, when five were being produced weekly. The standard version from the 501st helicopter has been the R22 Beta which introduced various improvements on the R22 Alpha, and this is available with floats (as illustrated) as the R22 Mariner. There is also a law enforcement version known as the R22 Police, this having been supplied to various law enforcement agencies, and various items of specialist equipment are available as options, including a load-carrying hook kit complete with electric and mechanical emergency releases.

SCHWEIZER 330 SKY KNIGHT

Country of Origin: USA.

Type: Three/four-seat light utility helicopter.

Power Plant: One 200 shp Allison 225-C10A turboshaft.

Performance: (At 2,050 lb/930 kg) Max cruise speed, 115 mph (185 km/h); normal cruise, 105 mph (169 km/h); hovering ceiling (in ground effect), 18,000 ft (5 485 m), (out of ground effect), 14,000 ft (4 265 m); max range (no reserves), 290 mls (466 km) at 4,000 ft (1 220 m).

Weights: Empty, 1,050 lb (476 kg); max take-off, 2,050 lb (930 kg), (with external load), 2,150 lb (975 kg).

Dimensions: Rotor diam, 26 ft 10 in (8,18 m); overall length, 30 ft 10 in (9,40 m).

Notes: The Model 330 Sky Knight, the prototype of which made its first public flight on 14 June 1988, uses most of the systems, controls, rotors and dynamic components of the piston-engined Model 300C purchased by Schweizer from the McDonnell Douglas Helicopter Company in November 1986. Apart from using a turboshaft, the Sky Knight differs from its predecessor in having a new, longer and wider forward fuselage. For the instructional role three seats are provided and flight controls may be fitted at all three seat positions. It is anticipated that the Sky Knight will be marketed for a variety of duties, including scout/observation, law enforcement, photography, light utility, VIP transportation and agricultural spraying. Marketing of the Sky Knight utility helicopter is expected to commence in 1990.

SIKORSKY H-53E

Country of Origin: USA.
Type: (CH-53E) Heavy duty transport and (MH-53E) mine counter measures helicopter.
Power Plant: Three 4,380 shp General Electric T64-GE-416 turboshafts.
Performance: (CH-53E at 56,000 lb/25 400 kg) Max speed, 196 mph (315 km/h) at sea level; max continuous cruise, 173 mph (278 km/h); max inclined climb (with 25,000-lb/11 340-kg payload), 2,500 ft/min (12,70 m/sec); service ceiling, 18,500 ft (5 640 m); hovering ceiling (in ground effect), 11,550 ft (3 520 m), (out of ground effect), 9,500 ft (2 895 m); unrefuelled range, 1,290 mls (2 075 km).
Weights: Empty (CH-53E) 33,228 lb (15 072 kg), (MH-53E) 36,336 lb (16 482 kg); max take-off (internal payload), 69,750 lb (31 640 kg), (external payload), 73,500 lb (33 340 kg).
Dimensions: Rotor diam, 79 ft 0 in (24,08 m); fuselage length, 73 ft 4 in (22,35 m).
Notes: A growth version of the twin-engined H-53D series, the H-53E first flew on 1 March 1974, and when production terminates in the 1990 Fiscal Year, the US Navy will have procured 15 CH-53E Super Stallion heavy duty transports and 32 MH-53E Sea Dragon mine countermeasures helicopters, and the US Marine Corps will have acquired 102 CH-53Es. The latter service operates the CH-53E in an amphibious assault role, and, although capable of carrying up to 55 fully-armed troops, its primary roles are transportation of heavy equipment and retrieval.

SIKORSKY UH-60A BLACK HAWK

Country of Origin: USA.
Type: Tactical transport helicopter.
Power Plant: Two 1,560 shp General Electric T700-GE-700 turboshafts.
Performance: (At 16,994 lb/7 708 kg) Max speed, 184 mph (296 km/h) at sea level; max cruise, 167 mph (268 km/h) at 4,000 ft (1 220 m); hovering ceiling (in ground effect), 9,500 ft (2 895 m), (out of ground effect), 5,600 ft (1 705 m); range (max internal fuel and 30 min reserves), 373 mls (600 km), (with two 230 US gal/870 l pylon tanks), 1,012 mls (1 630 km).
Weights: Empty, 11,284 lb (5 118 kg); max take-off, 22,000 lb (9 979 kg).
Dimensions: Rotor diam, 53 ft 8 in (16,23 m); fuselage length, 50 ft 0¾ in (15,26 m).
Notes: First flown on 17 October 1974, the UH-60A was designed to meet the US Army's UTTAS (Utility Tactical Transport System) requirement, and the service anticipates procuring a total of 2,253 helicopters of this type. Of these, nearly 1,200 were contracted for by the beginning of 1989, the 1,000th having been delivered in October 1988. WS-70 is the designation applied to the S-70A tactical utility version of the UH-60A assembled in the UK by Westland, which company is expected to supply some 80–90 to Saudi Arabia. Currently under development are the UH-60L and -60M, these being powered by the 1,857 shp T700-GE-701C turboshaft, the latter featuring a new all-composite rotor system.

SIKORSKY SH-60B SEAHAWK

Country of Origin: USA.
Type: Anti-submarine warfare and anti-ship surveillance and targeting helicopter.
Power Plant: Two 1,900 shp General Electric T700-GE-401C turboshafts.
Performance: (At 20,244 lb/9 183 kg) Max speed, 167 mph (269 km/h) at sea level; max cruise, 155 mph (249 km/h) at 5,000 ft (1 525 m); time on station (at radius of 57 mls/92 km), 3·86 hrs.
Weights: Empty (ASW mission), 13,648 lb (6 191 kg); normal take-off, 20,244 lb (9 182 kg), (ASST mission), 18,373 lb (8 334 kg), (utility), 21,884 lb (9 926 kg).
Dimensions: Rotor diam, 53 ft 8 in (16,36 m); fuselage length, 50 ft 0¾ in (15,26 m).
Notes: The S-70B was, as the SH-60B Seahawk, winner of the US Navy's LAMPS (Light Airborne Multi-Purpose System) Mk III helicopter contest, and the first of five prototypes flew on 12 December 1979. The first production SH-60B flew on 11 February 1983, with some 120 delivered by the beginning of 1989, when production was continuing at a rate of two monthly against a total US Navy requirement for 204 helicopters. Current developments include the SH-60F Ocean Hawk (intended to protect the inner zone of a carrier battle group), and the HH-60H and HH-60J, these being combat search and rescue and medium-range recovery helicopters for the US Navy and US Coast Guard respectively. The S-70B has been ordered by Australia and Japan.

SIKORSKY S-76B

Country of Origin: USA.
Type: Light commercial transport helicopter.
Power Plant: Two 960 shp Pratt & Whitney Canada PT6B-36 turboshafts.
Performance: (At 11,700 lb/5 307 kg) Max speed, 178 mph (287 km/h) at sea level; max cruise, 167 mph (269 km/h); econ cruise, 151 mph (243 km/h); max inclined climb, 1,500 ft/min (7,62 m/sec); hovering ceiling (in ground effect), 8,200 ft (2 500 m), (out of ground effect), 5,400 ft (1 646 m); range (standard fuel and 30 min reserves), 359 mls (578 km) at 150 mph (241 km/h) at 3,000 ft (915 m).
Weights: Empty, 6,548 lb (2,970 kg); max take-off, 11,700 lb (5 307 kg).
Dimensions: Rotor diam, 44 ft 0 in (13,41 m); fuselage length, 43 ft 4½ in (13,22 m).
Notes: The S-76B, which first flew on 22 June 1984, is a derivative of the S-76A Mk II which differs primarily in having two 650 shp Allison 250-C30S turboshafts. An engine option for the latter is the Turboméca Arriel 1S which is offered as a retrofit. The S-76B, which accommodates pilot and co-pilot plus a maximum of 12 passengers, offers a 51 per cent increase in useful load under hot and high conditions by comparison with the S-76A, and more than 300 S-76s were in service by the beginning of 1989. A more basic version is the S-76 Utility, and the H-76 Eagle is a military development for transport, gunship, assault, combat SAR, observation post and other roles.

WESTLAND SUPER LYNX

Country of Origin: United Kingdom.
Type: Multi-role maritime helicopter.
Power Plant: Two 1,120 shp Rolls-Royce Gem 42-1 turbo-shafts.
Performance: Max continuous cruise speed, 144 mph (232 km/h); max endurance speed, 81 mph (130 km/h); max inclined climb, 1,970 ft/min (10 m/sec); range (anti-surface vessel mission with four Stingray, Penguin or Sea Skua AShMs and 20 min reserves), 265 mls (426 km), (search and rescue), 391 mls (630 km).
Weights: Max take-off, 11,300 lb (5 126 kg).
Dimensions: Rotor diam, 42 ft 0 in (12,80 m); length (main rotor folded), 45 ft 3 in (13,79 m).
Notes: An export version of the British Navy's Lynx HAS Mk 3 helicopter the Super Lynx, 12 of which are being procured by the South Korean Navy, is equipped with Ferranti Sea Spray Mk 3 radar and BAe Sea Skua anti-ship missiles. In the rescue role, the Super Lynx accommodates eight survivors, three on casualty stretchers, and has a 600-lb (272-kg) hoist. A multi-role military assault equivalent of the Super Lynx is known as the Battlefield Lynx, this being capable of accommodating 12 fully-equipped troops and being intended for assault, anti-tank, armed escort and reconnaissance missions. On 11 August 1986, a Lynx demonstrator established an absolute speed record for helicopters with an average 249·09 mph (400·87 km/h), this having BERP III advanced technology main rotor blades.

INDEX OF AIRCRAFT TYPES

A-5K (Fantan), CNAMC, 80
Aérospatiale AS 332L Super Puma, 218
 AS 350B Ecureuil, 219
 AS 355F2 Ecureuil 2, 220
 Epsilon, 6
 SA 365N Dauphin 2, 221
Agusta A 109A, 222
 A 129 Mangusta, 223
AH-1F Cobra/TOW, Bell, 224
AH-1W SuperCobra, Bell, 225
AH-64A Apache, McDonnell Douglas, 239
Airbus A300–600, 8
 A310–300, 10
 A320–200, 12
Airtech CN-235–100, 14
 CN-260, 14
Alpha Jet 2, Dassault-Breguet/Dornier, 92
AMX International AMX, 16
Antonov An-32 (Cline), 18
 An-72 (Coaler), 20
 An-74 (Coaler), 20
 An-124 (Condor), 22
 An-225, 24
AStar Mk III, Aérospatiale AS 350D, 219
Atlantique 2, Dassault-Breguet, 84
ATP, British Aerospace, 54
ATR 42, 26
ATR 72, 26
AV-8B, McDonnell Douglas/BAe, 56
Avanti, Piaggio P.180, 170
Avtek 400A, 28

B-1B, Rockwell, 180
B-2, Northrop, 164
Backfire-C (Tu-26), Tupolev, 208
Beechcraft 2000 Starship 1, 32
 Beechjet 400A, 30
Beechjet 400A, Beechcraft, 28
Bell 214ST SuperTransport, 226
 222UT, 227
 406CS, 228
 412SP, 229

AH-1F Cobra/TOW, 224
AH-1W SuperCobra, 225
 /Boeing V-22 Osprey, 34
BK 117, MBB-Kawasaki, 236
Black Hawk, Sikorsky UH-60A, 249
Blackjack (Tu-160), 210
Boeing 737–500, 36
 747–400, 38
 757–200, 40
 767–300, 42
 Canada Dash 8–300, 46
 E-3 Sentry, 44
 Helicopters 414–100, 230
 Helicopters Chinook, 230
BO 105, MBB, 234
BO 108, MBB, 235
Brasilia, Embraer EMB-120, 96
British Aerospace 125–800, 48
 146–300, 50
 146STA, 52
 ATP, 54
 Harrier GR Mk 5, 56
 Hawk 100, 58
 Hawk 200, 60
 Jetstream Super 31, 62
 Sea Harrier FRS Mk 2, 64
Bromon BR-2000, 66

C-23A, Shorts, 190
C-29A, British Aerospace, 48
C-130 Hercules, Lockheed, 140
CAC F-7P Skybolt, 76
Canadair CL-215T, 70
 Challenger 601–3A, 68
Candid (Il-76), 124
Canguro, Siai Marchetti SF 600 TP, 198
CBA-123, Embraer-FAMA, 100
Cessna Citation 5, 74
 U-27A, 72
CH-47 Chinook, Boeing Helicopters, 230
CH-53E Super Stallion, Sikorsky, 248
Challenger 601–3A, Canadair, 68
Chengdu F-7P Skybolt, 76

Chinook, Boeing Helicopters CH-47, 230
Citation 5, Cessna, 74
Claudius Dornier Seastar, 78
Cline (An-32), 18
CNAMC A-5K (Fantan), 80
Coaler (An-72), 20
Cobra/TOW, Bell AH-1F, 224
Combat Scout, Bell 406CS, 228
Condor (An-124), 22
Convair Turbo-Firecat, 82
Corsair II, LTV YA-7F, 146

Dash 8–300, Boeing Canada, 46
Dassault-Breguet Atlantique 2, 84
    Mirage 2000N, 86
    Mystère-Falcon 900, 88
    Rafale A, 90
    /Dornier Alpha Jet 2, 92
Dauphin 2, Aérospatiale SA 365N, 221
Defender, McDonnell Douglas 530 MG/TOW, 238
Dolphin, Aérospatiale HH-65A, 221
Dornier Do 228–200, 94
    Seastar, Claudius, 78

E-3 Sentry, Boeing, 44
Eagle, McDonnell Douglas F-15E, 148
Eagle, Sikorsky H-76, 251
Ecureuil, Aérospatiale AS 350B, 219
Ecureuil 2, Aérospatiale AS 355, 220
EH Industries EH 101, 231
Embraer EMB-120 Brasilia, 96
    EMB-312 Tucano, 98
    -FAMA CBA-123, 100
ENAER T-35 Pillán, 102
Epsilon, Aérospatiale, 6

F-7P Skybolt, Chengdu, 76
F-14A (Plus) Tomcat, Grumman, 118
F-15E Eagle, McDonnell Douglas, 148
F-117A, Lockheed, 138
F/A-18 Hornet, McDonnell Douglas, 150
FAMA IA 63 Pampa, 104
Fantan (CNAMC A-5K), 80
Fencer (Su-24), 200
FFV/MFI BA-14 Starling, 106

Fighting Falcon, General Dynamics F-16, 114
Finback-B (SAC J-8 II), 188
Flanker-B (Su-27), 204
Fokker 50, 108
    100, 110
Foxhound (MiG-31), 162
Frogfoot (Su-25), 202
Fuji KM-2D, 112
Foxhound (MiG-31), 162
Fulcrum (MiG-29), 160

General Dynamics F-16, 114
Goshawk, McDonnell Douglas/BAe T-45A, 152
Gripen, Saab 39, 184
Grumman F-14A(Plus) Tomcat, 118
Gulfstream Aerospace Gulfstream SRA-4, 120
    /Swearingen SA-30, 122

H-76 Eagle, Sikorsky, 251
Halo (Mi-26), 243
Harrier GR Mk 5, BAe, 56
Hawk 100, BAe, 58
    200, BAe, 60
Havoc (Mi-28), 244
Haze (Mi-14), 240
Helix (Ka-27), 232
Hercules, Lockheed L-100–30, 140
Hermit (Mi-34), 245
Hind (Mi-24), 242
Hip (Mi-17), 241
Hornet, McDonnell Douglas F/A-18, 150

IA 63 Pampa, FAMA, 104
Ilyushin Il-76 (Candid), 124
    Il-78 (Midas), 124
    Il-96–300, 126
    Il-114, 128
Iskierka, PZL Mielec M-26, 176

Jaffe Aircraft SA-32T, 132
Jet Squalus, Promavia, 174
Jetstream Super 31, BAe, 62

Kamov Ka-27 (Helix), 232
  Ka-126, 233
Kawasaki T-4, 134

Laser 300, OMAC, 166
LET L 610, 136
Lockheed F-117A, 138
  L-100–30 Hercules, 140
  P-3C Orion, 142
  P-3 Sentinel, 144
LTV YA-7F Corsair II, 146
Lynx, Westland, 252

Mainstay (Ilyushin), 130
Mangusta, Augusta A 129, 223
MBB BO 105, 234
  BO 108, 235
  -Kawasaki BK 117, 236
McDonnell Douglas 500E, 237
  530MG/TOW Defender, 238
  AH-64A Apache, 239
  F-15E Eagle, 148
  F/A-18 Hornet, 150
  MD-11, 154
  MD-87, 156
  /BAe AV-8B Harrier II, 56
  /BAe T-45A Goshawk, 152
  /BAe TAV-8B Harrier II, 158
Midas (Il-78), 124
MH-53E Sea Dragon, Sikorsky, 248
Mikoyan MiG-29 (Fulcrum), 160
  MiG-31 (Foxhound), 162
Mil Mi-14 (Haze), 240
  Mi-17 (Hip), 241
  Mi-24 (Hind), 242
  Mi-25 (Hind), 242
  Mi-26 (Halo), 243
  Mi-28 (Havoc), 244
  Mi-34 (Hermit), 245
  Mi-35 (Hind), 242
Mirage 2000N, Dassault-Breguet, 86
Mriya, An-225, 24
Mystère-Falcon 900, Dassault-
  Breguet, 88

Northrop B-2, 164

OH-58D, Bell, 228
OMAC Laser 300, 166

Orion, Lockheed P-3C, 142
Orlik, PZL-130, 178
Osprey, Bell/Boeing V-22, 34

P-3C Orion, Lockheed, 142
Pampa, FAMA IA 63, 104
Panavia Tornado F Mk 3, 168
Piaggio P.180 Avanti, 170
Pilatus PC-9, 172
Pillán, ENAER T-35, 102
Promavia Jet Squalus, 174
PZL-130 Orlik, 178
PZL Mielec M-26 Iskierka, 176

Rafale A, Dassault-Breguet, 90
Redigo, Valmet L-90 TP, 214
Robinson R22, 246
Rockwell B-1B, 180
  /MBB X-31A, 182
Ruslan, Antonov An-124, 22

SA-30, Gulfstream/Swearingen, 122
SA-32T, Jaffe Aircraft, 132
Saab 39 Gripen, 184
  340, 186
SAC (Shenyang) J-8 II (Finback-B),
  188
Schweizer 330 Sky Knight, 247
Sea Dragon, Sikorsky MH-53E, 248
Sea Harrier RFS Mk 2, BAe, 64
Seahawk, Sikorsky SH-60B, 250
Seastar, Claudius Dornier, 78
Sentinel, Lockheed P-3, 144
SH-60B Seahawk, Sikorsky, 250
Shenyang (SAC) J-8 II (Finback-B),
  188
Sherpa, Shorts, 190
Shorts 360–300, 192
  S312 Tucano, 194
  Sherpa, 190
Siai Marchetti S.211, 196
SF 600TP Canguro, 198
Sikorsky H-53E, 248
  H-76 Eagle, 251
  S-76B, 251
  SH-60B Seahawk, 250
  UH-60A Black Hawk, 249
Skybolt, Chengdu F-7P, 76

Sky Knight, Schweizer 330, 247
SRA-4, Gulfstream, 120
Starling, FFV/MFI BA-14, 106
Starship, Beechcraft 2000, 32
Sukhoi Su-24 (Fencer), 200
 Su-25 (Frogfoot), 202
 Su-27 (Flanker-B), 204
SuperCobra, Bell AH-1W, 225
Super Lynx, Westland, 252
Super Puma, Aérospatiale AS 332L, 218
Super Stallion, Sikorsky CH-53E, 248
SuperTransport, Bell 214ST, 226

T-45A Goshawk, McDonnell Douglas/BAe, 152
TAV-8B Harrier II, McDonnell Douglas/BAe, 158
TBM International TBM 700, 206
Tomcat, Grumman F-14A (Plus), 118
Tornado F Mk 3, Panavia, 168

Tucano, Embraer EMB-312, 98
 Shorts S312, 194
Tupolev Tu-26 (Backfire-C), 208
 Tu-160 (Blackjack-A), 210
 Tu-204, 212
Turbo-Firecat, Convair, 82
TwinStar, Aérospatiale AS 355, 220

U-27A, Cessna, 72
UH-60A Back Hawk, Sikorsky, 249

V-22 Osprey, Bell/Boeing, 34
Valmet L-90 TP Redigo, 214

Westland Super Lynx, 252

X-31A, Rockwell/MBB, 182
XAC (Xian) H-7, 216

YA-7F Corsair II, LTV, 146